"I'm not going to sleep with you!"

Rachel ignored his amused grin. "I'm going along with you because you've been kind to Jacey. But I won't go to bed with you."

"I don't believe I asked for such a sacrifice."

"But those looks you've been giving me..."

John stepped toward her. "I'm attracted to you. You feel it, too, don't you?" He slid a finger down her cheek. "I wouldn't complain if you lured me upstairs this minute. But that's not what our agreement is about."

"No, it's not." Weakness hit her knees.

"Your cheeks are red again," he murmured.

She knew why. No clothes could hide the strength of his shoulders, his muscular legs. Nor the warmth in his eyes when he smiled at her child, or the silent offer to protect the two of them against the world.

He was playing the role of Knight in Shining Armor.

It was incredibly seductive. And completely unbelievable.

Dear Reader,

American Romance cordially invites you to a wedding of convenience. By popular demand, we're continuing our special series, IN NAME ONLY, where couples marry first and love later.

Judy Christenberry brings you this pair of reluctant newlyweds: John Crewes and Rachel Cason. When Rachel's precocious daughter "buys" herself a daddy, she buys her mommy a husband, too!

We hope you enjoy this and all the IN NAME ONLY books coming to you in the months ahead.

Regards,

Debra Matteucci
Senior Editor & Editorial Coordinator
Harlequin Books
300 E. 42nd St.
New York, NY 10017

Judy Christenberry

DADDY ON DEMAND

Harlequin Books

TORONTO • NEW YORK • LONDON
AMSTERDAM • PARIS • SYDNEY • HAMBURG
STOCKHOLM • ATHENS • TOKYO • MILAN
MADRID • WARSAW • BUDAPEST • AUCKLAND

ISBN 0-373-16626-5

DADDY ON DEMAND

Copyright © 1996 by Judy Christenberry

Chapter One

"I got money."

John Crewes looked up in surprise. He was stretched out on a lounger on his carefully-maintained patio, looking forward to a relaxing afternoon. His plans had not included children. Specifically, the child hanging over the fence.

"Who are you? And what are you doing invading my peace and quiet?" he demanded.

"I want to have a business discussion," she pronounced with all the poise of a bank president.

He turned back to the *Wall Street Journal*. It made no difference to him if she discussed the downfall of capitalism. As long as she didn't bother him. "Fine. Just go away."

"No, with you," she protested. "I got money."

"Why do you keep saying that?"

"'Cause I want to hire you."

That got his attention. He was a financial expert; some said, a genius. This child wanted investment advice? Suddenly he remembered where he'd seen her. She lived next door. She and her mother had moved in at the beginning of the school year.

"Where's your mother?"

"Shh!" she warned, panic on her face. "Don't tell her."

"I don't think I should help you do something your mother doesn't approve of."

"It's my money. She says I can spend it however I want, as long as it's not bad."

Her determination amused him. "Do you want to come over?" He didn't know what she was standing on, but her little snub nose just topped the fence.

"Yes."

Her face immediately disappeared from view. He heard a rustling noise as she ran from his fence to the gate, then the creak of the latch. He needed to oil it. Nothing squeaked or was out of place on his property.

She came into view—a little girl dressed in shorts and a T-shirt, with grubby knees and a streak of dirt on her cheek. Her dark brown hair was in a scraggly ponytail. Coming to a halt beside his chair, she suddenly showed signs of bashfulness.

He rested the newspaper in his lap and crossed his arms over his chest. "Well, now, what kind of advice do you want?"

She frowned, putting one slightly smudged finger to her rosebud lips. "No. Not that. I don't want you to talk to me. I want to hire you. I got money."

Amused by her persistence, he replied, "I don't do lawns anymore. Maybe you'd better get your mom to help you."

"No. She can't. She's a girl."

Tears would have irritated him. But the sadness in her eyes touched something inside him. "Has to be a guy, huh? Okay, what do you need?"

"A daddy."

She watched him as if he were a prized specimen under a microscope. She was lucky he hadn't choked.

"Sorry, honey, but you're out of luck. I'm not interested in marriage." Understatement of the year. He'd tried that celebrated institution once and hadn't fared so well. He kept his social commitments to the strictly temporary kind now.

"Me, neither."

He was beginning to think a friend was playing a practical joke on him. "That's good. You're a little young to consider tying yourself down."

"But I need a daddy."

"I think you need to discuss this with your mommy."

The little girl licked her lips before saying, "Nope. Mommy says we don't need no men. We're just two girls on our own."

"Ah. Well, then, I guess you don't need a daddy."

"Yes, I do. I'm tired of being the only one."

"The only one what?"

As if she thought he really cared, she settled on the edge of his recliner. "All the other kids have daddies."

"I'm sure that's not true. As many people as get divorced these days, there have to be other kids in your class without daddies."

"Lisbeth's mommy found her a daddy. That only leaves Earl and me, and he doesn't count."

"Why?"

"'Cause he doesn't care."

"Look—" He broke off. "What is your name?"

"Jacey."

"Okay, Jacey, this problem is between you and your mother. If Lisbeth's mommy can find a daddy, I'm

sure your mommy can, too." In fact, from what he'd
seen of her mommy—from a distance, of course—he
suspected she could find any number of daddies. She
had long dark hair, a curvaceous figure and full, pouty
lips that begged to be kissed. Not that he'd noticed.

"'Course she could," Jacey agreed. "But she don't
want one."

Why did he feel like he was spinning his wheels?
This conversation didn't seem to be going anywhere
and he still hadn't even read the headlines of the paper.

"Well, I need to read my paper now, Jacey. So why
don't you go back to your yard and play."

She stood and John breathed a sigh of relief. He
hadn't thought it would be that easy to get her to go
away. Instead of leaving, however, she slid her hand
into a pocket and pulled out a small cloth bag. Even
as he watched, she struggled to untie the string that
held the bag closed.

"What are you doing?"

"I'm showing you my money. I told you I got
money."

"Yes, you did, but I don't understand—"

"I want to hire you. To be my daddy."

That stubborn tilt to her little chin found a spot of
warmth in his soul. She'd go a long way in life. But not
with him. "That's not a job you can hire someone
for."

"Why not? It'd just be once in a while."

"What are you talking about?"

She sat back down on the edge of the recliner and
patted his blue jeans-clad leg. "It wouldn't be very
hard."

"What wouldn't be very hard?"

"Telling the other kids about your job. You could tell'm about capturing the bad guys and shooting guns and—"

"Whoa! Wait just a minute. I'm not a policeman."

The disappointment on her face struck hard.

"Oh. I thought maybe— Do you fight fires and ride a fire engine?" Her voice rose on a hopeful note.

"Sorry, sweetheart. I'm in finance."

"What's that?"

"I invest people's money and make it grow for them."

He could tell she wasn't impressed. Suddenly she leaned forward and patted his cheek with her soft, pudgy little hand. "That's okay. They'll like you anyway."

An unexpected grin forced his lips to curve up. What a kid. "Thanks for the reassurance, but I can't—"

"But it wouldn't take long. The daddies don't stay all day. And besides," she said, her face taking on a hangdog air, "I told'm you'd come."

Ah. Now they'd come to the crux of the matter. "Jacey, I'm afraid you'll just have to tell your teacher you weren't honest."

"I got three dollars and sixty-seven cents," she hurriedly said and began struggling with the opening of her bag again.

"Jacey—"

"Isn't that enough?" The anxious look on her face bothered him.

"Look, sweetheart, your mom would find out about it, and you'd get in trouble."

"No, she won't. She's not at my school. See, I could hire you for—for the rest of school. Then, next year, I'd just say you left, like Earl's daddy did."

He had to admit she had everything figured out. There was only about a month left of school. Even though he told himself he shouldn't, he asked, "Just when are the daddies supposed to speak at your school?"

"Monday morning."

He got his second wind. "Jacey, I don't think—"

"I'll get my allowance next Friday. I'll have a whole 'nother dollar. I'll give that to you, too." The desperation in her voice reminded him how much things mattered when you were a kid.

"How about if I discuss this with your mother?"

"No! It would make her sad. She says we don't need no boys." Big blue eyes stared at him. "But I *do*. Just every once in a while, so's I can be like the other kids."

He remembered how important it was to fit in. When he was eight and on his first baseball team, he'd died of embarrassment when it was his turn to provide refreshments. His mother had arrived in heels and pearls with a bakery box of petits fours. The other boys had goggled at her as she'd passed out dainty napkins. How he'd longed for homemade cookies and a blue jeans-clad mom like the other kids.

Hell, what could it hurt if he went along with Jacey's plan? She was a cute little urchin and he didn't have a full calendar Monday. "Okay. But only this once, okay?"

"No," she immediately responded, that stubborn chin in evidence again. "You have to do it 'til school's finished. Not all the time, just when I need you." She held out her bag of money. "It's a lot of money."

He guessed it was a lot of money to Jacey. Reaching out for the cloth bag, he said, "Okay, just when you need me."

"Thank you," she said, beaming at him. Then she launched herself on his chest, smacked his cheek and ran away.

Only when he was alone again did he realize he didn't know the name of her school or the time he was to appear.

He'd wait until tomorrow to see if she returned to give him the information he needed. If not, he guessed he'd have to pay his beautiful, independent, "We don't need no boys" neighbor a visit.

RACHEL CASON SCRUBBED the sink with a vengeance. A navy blue stain encircled the white porcelain. *That's what you get for trying to save money, Rachel,* she said to herself. She'd dyed a pale blue dress with stains to a navy blue, hoping to stretch another year's wear out of it.

Now she had extra work, trying to remove the dye stains from the sink.

The back door slammed. "Jacey?"

"Yes, Mommy. I'm here."

She looked over her shoulder at the bundle of energy that was the center of her universe and grinned. "Hi, sweetheart. Ooh, I can see you've been having fun, but you're quite a mess. I think you'd better have a bath before dinner tonight. Go get clean pajamas and—" The phone rang. "Oh, answer that first, sweetheart."

Jacey climbed up on the stool by the wallphone and lifted the receiver. "Cason residence."

Rachel smiled. Her daughter was so self-possessed it scared her sometimes.

"It's for you, Mommy."

Rachel took the receiver automatically, but her gaze registered the look of alarm on Jacey's face. "Hello?"

"Mrs. Cason? Of course, that's not your name now, but I don't have time to visit tonight. I'm already late as it is. This is Mrs. Wilson. I just wanted you to tell your husband to be at school at nine-thirty Monday. He's going to be the second daddy. Thanks so much. Bye."

Rachel stood there with the receiver in her hand until the beeping alerted her to hang it up. Then she turned to her small daughter, who was still staring up at her, her eyes abnormally large with fear.

"Maybe you can explain that phone call, young lady."

"Who was it?"

"I think you know. It was Mrs. Wilson, your kindergarten teacher."

"I did good on my work, Mommy."

"You always do, sweetheart. But this wasn't about your work. It was about your daddy."

If anything, those eyes grew even bigger. "I don't *have* a daddy, Mommy. Don't you remember?"

Rachel studied her child, wondering exactly what was going on. "I remember, and I believe you remember. Why doesn't Mrs. Wilson remember?"

"She probably mixed me up with Lisbeth. Did I tell you Lisbeth got a daddy?"

For the first time, Rachel noticed a touch of forlornness in her daughter's expression. She knelt down to put her arms around Jacey. "Yes, you told me. Does it make you want a daddy?"

"No!" Jacey squeezed her neck tightly. "It's just you and me, Mommy."

"That's right. Just you and me, kid, and we're doing fine."

Jacey pulled back from their hug. "I'll go take my bath now, Mommy. I don't want to go to bed late."

Jacey might be smart—brilliant, in fact, as her teacher had told Rachel at Christmas—but thankfully she was woefully inadequate at lying.

"That's very good of you, Jacey, but first I think you ought to explain why Mrs. Wilson thinks you have a daddy."

"Oh." Jacey stared at her toes, one little forefinger between her teeth. When Rachel said nothing, she finally looked at her mother. "I said I had a daddy."

"Why did you do that?"

"'Cause I was tired of all the others daddies coming and telling us about their work. Now, even Lisbeth's daddy is coming."

Rachel nodded. "I understand why you might be disappointed, but you shouldn't lie. Would you like me to come tell the kids about *my* job?"

Jacey's solemn little face broke into a gentle smile. "Thank you, Mommy, but you're a teacher. We know all about teachers."

"Ah. And what were you going to do Monday morning when your new daddy didn't show up?"

"Oh, he would be— Uh, I don't know."

"He would what?" Rachel demanded. She knew her daughter very well. A more practical five-year-old didn't exist. "Jacey, what have you done?"

"I used my own money."

"Money? What are you talking about?"

"I hired me a daddy. Just 'til summer, Mommy."

"Your savings? You used your money to hire a daddy?" She couldn't believe what she was hearing. "Just how much money have you saved?"

"Three dollars and sixty-seven cents."

Great. What kind of a sleaze would take money from a child and promise such a ridiculous thing? "And who did you hire?"

"Him." Jacey accompanied her one-word answer with a gesture toward the house next door. The house in which, according to neighborhood gossip, a financial genius lived. A single financial genius.

Several times Polly, her neighbor across the street, had offered to set Rachel up with the man. She couldn't remember what Polly had called him, and it didn't matter. Each time she'd refused.

The divorcée next door to Polly had pursued the man for a while, but she had conceded defeat, telling her neighbors that he was a cold fish. Mr. Donaldson, the head of the neighborhood group, had agreed, reporting the man had no interest in attending their meetings, or helping them in their efforts to fight crime and littering.

This was the warmhearted soul who'd taken her baby's savings and offered to pretend to be Jacey's daddy?

"You hired our neighbor to be your daddy? He actually agreed to such an insane proposal?" She regretted her words as soon as they were out. She never made fun of Jacey.

Jacey took her words literally. "No, Mommy, he said he didn't want to marry you."

Hysterical laughter bubbled up in Rachel and she bit her bottom lip. "Well, I'm grateful for that, at least.

I think you would've paid too much if marriage was included."

"Me, too," Jacey agreed, nodding sagely. "He should pay *us* to marry us."

Leave it to Jacey to carry the concept too far. Rachel needed to do some backtracking. "Sweetie, you don't use money for—for marrying and things. You're only supposed to do those things because of love."

"Oh. Then I'm glad he didn't want to marry you."

Rachel wished Jacey would quit repeating that fact.

She stood and held out her hand. "Come on, Jacey. We've got to go clear things up with that man. I'm afraid he can't pretend to be your father Monday morning."

Jacey put her small hand in her mother's but she didn't try to hide her unhappiness. "But, Mommy, I *paid* him!"

"Too bad, sweetie. You just lost your savings."

JOHN WAS WATCHING the last holes of a golf championship on television, enjoying the first free day he'd taken in a long time. He'd become a workaholic after his divorce, and it had paid handsomely. But lately, he wasn't finding the frenetic pace as satisfying.

In fact, Jacey's visit this afternoon was the most interesting thing, other than making money, that had happened to him in a long time. He began mentally preparing his speech to the children. After all, he didn't want to let Jacey down. It was bad enough that he wasn't a policeman or a fireman.

Inspiration suddenly struck him and he hurried to the storage closet. With every box neatly stacked and labeled, it took only seconds to find the one he was looking for.

The doorbell rang as he carried the box back to the den. Setting it down, he impatiently strode to the door. It could only be a salesman. He'd already bought several boxes of Girl Scout cookies, and he avoided his neighbors, especially the neighborhood kingpin, Donaldson. The man persisted in trying to get John to attend those meetings. The thought of spending several hours discussing lawn beautification over lemonade and cookies drove him crazy.

The one neighbor he hadn't avoided that day, Jacey, stood at his door with the beautiful woman he'd seen only from a distance. Up close, she was a knockout.

At least, she would be if she smiled, he was sure. She wasn't smiling now.

"Hello, Jacey," he said and looked pointedly at the woman.

"I'm afraid I don't know your name, but I'm Rachel Cason," she said, her nose in the air. "I understand you and my daughter made an agreement today."

"John Crewes," he said, extending his hand, which she pointedly ignored. "Won't you come in?"

"That won't be necessary. I apologize for Jacey interrupting your day. And, of course, the agreement is null and void."

Jacey pulled on her mother's arm. "What's null and void, Mommy?"

"It means that Mr. Crewes won't be pretending to be your daddy Monday morning."

He noticed her voice warmed considerably as she talked to her daughter, even though she sounded very strict. Good. He wanted Jacey to have someone who loved her. Although it was none of his business, of course.

"Well, Mrs. Cason," he began, waiting until her gaze returned to him before he continued, "I promised Jacey, and I don't like to go back on my word." He smiled at her, determined to see if he could thaw her out just a little. After all, he'd been told his smile was attractive.

Nada. Zip. Nothing.

"I appreciate your feelings, Mr. Crewes, but, as Jacey's mother, I can't condone lying."

He looked down at Jacey, her hand held by her mother. She was staring up at him, not crying, just looking, accepting, wishing.

Clearing his throat, he said, "Can't we find a compromise?" What was the matter with him? he wondered. Here he was being offered a way out of a ridiculous situation and he wasn't taking it.

"I really don't see—"

"If you'd come inside, we could at least explore the options. After all, I've already been paid. It hardly seems fair to make me return such an enormous windfall."

His attempt at levity was almost ignored. The corners of her tempting lips quivered just slightly. He was mesmerized even though she quickly flattened them out into a stern line.

"There's no need to return Jacey's money. It will teach her not to make such poor decisions in the future."

"Man, you are one tough bird. How do you stand living with her, Jacey?"

Jacey gave him a shy smile and leaned against her mother's leg. "She's my mommy," she explained.

The woman looked down at her child and then at him. "Why do I get the feeling I'm being ganged up on?"

"Why, Mrs. Cason, I have no idea," he said in tones of mock amazement. The lightheartedness that filled him was a surprise. Usually, he played the heavy, whether it was with his employees or clients importuning him. That was something else he was tiring of.

"What big eyes you have, Grandma," she returned, narrowing her gaze in speculation.

"The better to see you with when you accept my invitation and come inside." He watched exasperation, and maybe something else if he was very optimistic, fill her gaze before he added, "Come on. What can it hurt if we discuss this a little, explore our options?"

"Please, Mommy?" Jacey whispered, sending imploring glances to her mother.

"Definitely ganged up on," her mother muttered before giving a nod. "Very well. But nothing you do or say will get me to agree to your telling Mrs. Wilson that you are Jacey's father."

Chapter Two

Jacey watched the clock as she nibbled on her finger. Lisbeth's father was speaking to the class, but Jacey wasn't interested. No, she was waiting for John.

Her pretend daddy.

She swallowed the bad feelings that filled her tummy. She and John had convinced her mommy to let John come to school today. But she was supposed to tell her teacher that John was just a friend, not her daddy.

Supposed to.

"I was going to," she muttered under her breath and received a frown from Mrs. Wilson. But she wanted to wait until John got here. Somehow, with him beside her, telling the truth wouldn't seem so difficult. But he hadn't come.

"He promised," she whispered to herself, fighting back the tears. Daddies were supposed to keep their promises.

When the students around her began clapping, Jacey did, too, but the applause made her feel even worse. It was time for her father to talk. Not only did she not have a father, she didn't even have a pretend father.

"That was lovely, Mr. Wester. I admire your work tremendously," Mrs. Wilson said, smiling at Lisbeth's daddy. There was a pause in the room, like everyone was waiting for the show to continue, Jacey thought to herself.

She raised troubled eyes to look at her teacher. Mrs. Wilson was staring at her, a question in her gaze.

Before Jacey could come up with an excuse, the door to the classroom swung open. There he was!

Jacey grinned from ear to ear. Without conscious thought, she leaped from her desk and raced to the back of the room, throwing her arms around his legs and hugging as hard as she could.

"Sorry, baby," he murmured. "I got held up on a phone call."

Baby. She was a big girl, as she told her mommy all the time, but she decided she didn't mind *him* calling her a baby. It felt . . . nice. "That's okay."

"Mr. Crewes," Mrs. Wilson said, having walked to the back of the room to meet him and extending her hand. "If you'll come forward, I'm afraid you'll have to start at once. We have reading circles in a few minutes, and we wouldn't want to get off schedule, now, would we?"

John looked at Jacey, and she knew what he wanted to know. Had she told her teacher he was a friend, not a daddy? Her finger went back to her mouth and she barely shook her head no. She knew he understood because he looked unhappy, like *his* tummy didn't feel too good, either.

She returned to her desk and screwed her eyes tightly shut. *Please, please, please . . .*

"Class, I want you to welcome John Crewes, Jacey's new daddy."

The class applauded, as Mrs. Wilson had told them to, but Jacey just stared at the tall man standing beside her teacher.

HELL! WHAT WAS HE supposed to do now? Rachel had told Jacey to explain to her teacher before John got there. Which seemed pretty tough to him. But Rachel had made them both promise that they'd be honest with the teacher.

But being honest with the teacher in private and being honest with the teacher in front of sixteen kindergartners were two different things. Especially when one of them was pleading with big blue eyes.

Eyes just like her mother's.

"Now, don't be nervous, Mr. Crewes," Mrs. Wilson prompted, gesturing to his audience.

Nervous? No, he wasn't nervous about his presentation. He'd rehearsed it in front of his mirror yesterday afternoon. The only thing that made him nervous was facing Rachel if she found out he hadn't explained.

He cleared his throat. He would come clean after his talk.

"Good morning. Jacey asked me to tell you about my job."

He smiled at the little girl, reassuring her, and her face lit up. Man, he was a sucker for her smile.

"I deal in money, but I'm not a banker. I take other people's money." He paused, leaning forward to touch the ear of the little boy nearest him, and held up a coin. "Like this boy's money. This is your money, isn't it?" he asked.

"No! I don't have no money!" the child protested.

"Then this isn't your money, either?" he asked, pulling a coin from the boy's other ear.

"Where's that comin' from?" the boy asked, covering his ears with his hands, and the class roared with laughter.

"Oh. Well, just pretend it's your money. You see, kids, if you have money, you want to save it for the future. But it would be good if, while you were saving it, your money made more money. So, my job is to take your money—" he held out the two coins and then put his hands behind his back "—and make it grow."

He extended his hands to show four coins. "And grow," he added, returning his hands behind his back and extending them again to show eight coins, to great applause from his small audience, and then repeated the process until there were sixteen quarters.

After he passed out a quarter to each of the children, he did a few more tricks, tying them in with money management, although he doubted the kids cared about his job.

"Where's your rabbit?" one little boy called out. Even Jacey's eyes lit up at that idea, but John shook his head. "Sorry. My rabbit is out of town. Any other questions?"

There were no questions but a lot of applause. The best reward he received, though, was the approval shining in Jacey's eyes.

"That was marvelous, Mr. Crewes," Mrs. Wilson said, walking forward. "We didn't know we'd get a magic show as well as an informative talk. Thank you so much for coming." She shook his hand.

Just as he was going to ask to speak to her alone, she looked over his shoulder and said, "And you, too, Mr. Wester. I'm so impressed with your career."

John turned around, a sinking feeling in his stomach. Yep, he was right. Mr. Wester was David Wester, a well-known psychologist who, for the past ten years, had been raking in money hand over fist, first with his books on relationships and then his videos showing how to make a marriage stronger.

The man, at least ten years older than John, with gray hair mixing with blond, extended his hand. "I enjoyed your talk as much as the children, Mr. Crewes. Which little girl is yours?"

"Uh, Jacey," John replied, just as a small hand slid into his. "Hi, sweetheart. Was it okay?"

He bent down and scooped Jacey up into his arms. She hugged his neck. "It was perfect, John."

Returning the kiss she'd given him on Saturday, he almost forgot the powerful man standing beside him. Almost.

"Hello, Jacey," David Wester said, as he was joined by Lisbeth. "I believe you and Lisbeth are best friends."

The two little girls nodded.

"Well, I'm especially glad to meet you, John, if I may call you that," the man continued. "I believe it's important to know the families of your child's playmates."

"Uh, yeah, that's a good idea."

"Well, thank you both for coming, but it's reading-circle time. We mustn't get off schedule, you know," Mrs. Wilson said. "Back to your desks, girls."

Jacey hugged his neck again, taking the opportunity to whisper, "I didn't tell her."

"I know," John whispered back. He set Jacey down and she scampered to her desk under Mrs. Wilson's stern eye. "Uh, Mrs. Wilson, could I talk to you for a minute?" he asked, hoping David Wester would leave before he made his confession.

"I'd love to have a visit with you and your wife, Mr. Crewes, but I can't stop right now. You understand, don't you? Even schoolteachers have busy schedules. Call me for an appointment. Thank you again for coming."

The woman walked back to the head of the class and began instructing her pupils.

With a sigh, John turned toward the door, only to find David Wester waiting for him.

"You know, I could buy and sell this entire school without the blink of an eye. But a schoolteacher can reduce me to a tongue-tied student in no time. Mothers and teachers must have some kind of special magic," he finished with a smile.

John couldn't agree more. And he knew one mother and teacher who seemed to have incredible power over him. "Yeah, they must."

Outside the building, David Wester shook his hand again and repeated how much he'd enjoyed John's talk and then each got in his own car and drove away.

On the way back to his office, John had a lot to think about. First of all, there was the satisfaction he'd gotten from pleasing Jacey. She was a sweetheart. He hadn't spent much time around kids. He'd been afraid he'd be even more out of place than his mother with her pearls and petits fours. That was when he'd hit on the magic he'd practiced religiously as a teenager to get over his shyness.

He was glad it had worked for Jacey.

Meeting David Wester was food for thought, too. He'd approached Wester's company once as a potential client, but Wester's assistant had assured him they were happy with their financial adviser. He didn't even know who represented Wester, but whoever it was, he was making a fortune.

What a surprise that Lisbeth's new daddy was David Wester. He was glad the man wasn't his client. That made one less person to whom he would have to explain his lie.

At least that had worked out okay.

Rachel wasn't going to be happy with him. That thought was almost as disturbing as Jacey's approval was pleasing. He had promised to straighten out the lie Jacey had told. Well, he and Jacey had promised. Rachel wasn't going to let Jacey off easy, either.

But she wouldn't refuse to speak to Jacey.

He suspected she might never speak to him again.

The hollowness such a thought brought disturbed him. He didn't need any woman. And had promised himself he never would again. His first wife had almost bankrupted him and ruined his business. He was through with women.

Except Jacey.

Rachel was another matter. He'd found himself wanting to touch her; had wanted to from the moment he'd opened his door to find her standing there. The half hour they'd spent negotiating his appearance this morning had only intensified that odd, compelling longing.

The way she handled Jacey, lovingly but firmly, had impressed him. The way she'd shifted in her chair when she was thinking drove him crazy. She'd worn jeans and a T-shirt that had clung to her curves. Generous curves... Well, generous in some places—the places that counted.

He licked his lips, finding them suddenly dry. Without question, he needed to avoid Rachel Cason.

Somehow, he didn't think that would be a problem when she found out what had happened.

RACHEL PULLED INTO the driveway of the child-care center where Jacey stayed after her morning kindergarten. She was a few minutes early, but she was anxious to see if Jacey had been hurt by her revelation that morning. She didn't want her child to suffer, but she also didn't want her to get away with a lie. There was an important lesson to be learned here.

She reached the door of Jacey's room and searched with her eyes for her daughter.

Obviously Jacey hadn't suffered too much. She was playing house with several little girls, pretending to cook something on the toy stove, giggling with the others.

"Oh, Mrs. Cason, you're here," the worker said, noticing Rachel for the first time.

Jacey heard her mother's name and dropped everything to come running. "You're here early, Mommy!"

Rachel hugged her, reveling in the little-girl smell, a combination of juice, cookies and pure sweetness. "Just a little, Jacey. Are you ready?"

"I have to put away my toys," Jacey explained and hurried back to her friends.

"Your little girl is so good. She's never a bit of trouble," the worker said, beaming at Jacey.

"Thank you," Rachel murmured, thinking about the mess Jacey had created this past weekend with her hiring of John Crewes. He was the kind of man Rachel avoided. Attractive, powerful, self-centered. At least, according to the divorcée and Mr. Donaldson.

"Ready, Mommy," Jacey announced, interrupting Rachel's thoughts.

Once the two of them were in the car, driving home, Rachel asked the question that had been on her mind all day. "So, how did Mr. Crewes do this morning? He did come, didn't he?"

"Oh, yes. He did magic tricks. And look," Jacey said, digging beneath the seat belt into the pocket in her shorts. She held her hand out to her mother and Rachel glanced down briefly before returning her gaze to the road.

"He gave you money?"

"He gave all of us a quarter! After he pulled it from behind Bobby's ear! Then he put it behind his back and made more money! Isn't that neat? I didn't know anyone could make money like that. If you learned how to do his trick, then you could stop working and stay home with me!"

Oh, great! Thanks to John Crewes she was learning that her daughter wanted a daddy and didn't want her mother to work. She owed the man a big thank-you! Maybe she could repay him by running over him. She didn't need this!

"Sweetie, you know I have to work in the summers to pay off my school loan. This is the last time, and then I won't have to teach summer school. We'll be able to be lazy together."

Jacey leaned over to pat her mother's arm, reassuringly. "I know, Mommy. I just thought it would be fun."

"Of course it would, angel. But what Mr. Crewes did was a magic trick. He didn't really make all those quarters."

"He didn't?"

Rachel sighed. "No, he didn't." Okay, so now she was bursting another of Jacey's bubbles. Chalk up something else she owed dear John. Maybe running over him was too nice.

"Oh." Jacey's little face reflected the same emotions she'd shown when she'd asked about Santa Claus. Rachel had hated to tell her this past Christmas that Santa was make-believe. But she'd always been honest with her child.

And Jacey had gotten over her disappointment. At least, it hadn't stopped her from enjoying her presents. She'd get over this disappointment, also. Especially if she didn't see John Crewes again.

"How about if you watch some cartoons for an hour, and then we go to McDonald's for dinner." She tried to save Jacey's favorite fast food for a special treat. Tonight, Jacey needed something to make up for her disappointment.

"Okay," the child agreed, a smile returning to her face.

And that hour of cartoons would give Rachel time to unwind, from both her teaching and the worry she'd had all day about Jacey and John Crewes.

As Rachel slipped into jeans and a knit shirt, she realized she hadn't asked Jacey what Mrs. Wilson's reaction had been. Oh, well, she'd get the nitty-gritty over dinner, when Jacey had her favorite food to distract her.

In the meantime, Rachel would fantasize about the punishment she'd wish on John Crewes's head for encouraging Jacey to believe in a fantasy even more far-fetched than Santa Claus.

JOHN LEFT WORK EARLY, shocking his staff. Normally, he was the last out of the office, usually finishing up at around eight or nine. He'd stop at a favorite restaurant and eat dinner on the way home. Then he'd work out with weights in his basement, read some financial reports, and go to bed at eleven.

Not an exciting life. But productive.

Today, he was anxious to be there for Jacey when the child told her mother she hadn't corrected her lie. After all, he was just as guilty. He would shoulder the blame for the little girl, shield her from her mother's disapproval. It was the honorable thing to do.

He whipped into his driveway, loosening his tie and unbuttoning the top button with one hand. He couldn't see any sign of life in the house next door, but an old Chevrolet compact car was in the driveway. He'd seen it before.

Grabbing his briefcase, he rushed into his house and up the stairs. In two minutes he'd discarded his suit and slipped on jeans, a shirt and tennis shoes.

In one minute flat he was down the stairs, out of the house and standing over on Rachel's front porch, pressing her doorbell. He was in a hurry because he wanted to protect Jacey. Not because he was anxious to see Rachel.

Not at all.

Almost at once the door opened and both ladies were standing in front of him.

Jacey beamed at him but said nothing. Rachel blinked several times, as if in surprise, then said, "Yes?"

She didn't look happy with him, but she also didn't appear ready to kill him. He glanced down at Jacey and received the merest hint of a headshake.

"Uh—" He stalled, wondering if it was possible that Jacey hadn't explained what had happened.

"Yes?" Rachel repeated.

For the first time, he noticed that she had her purse with her. "Were you on your way out?"

"We're going to McDonald's," Jacey announced, still beaming. "You want to come, too?"

"Jacey!" Rachel exploded, frowning at her child.

"Hey, I'd like that, Jacey, if your mom doesn't mind?" He looked at Rachel, waiting for her approval. His earlier idea of being there for Jacey made dinner a good idea. The way his heart thumped in overtime just looking at Rachel should have had him thinking the opposite, but it didn't.

Of course, he wasn't going to force his way in where he wasn't wanted, but...he put as much begging in his gaze as Jacey was putting in hers.

"You're ganging up on me again!" Rachel protested, looking at first one of them and then the other, fighting a smile.

"It'll be fun, Mommy," Jacey assured her.

"My treat," John offered as an inducement.

He realized he'd made a mistake almost at once. Rachel stiffened and her gaze froze him. "Jacey and I pay our own way. Bribery is not acceptable."

"Bribery? Hell, I— I mean, heck," he quickly amended when Rachel's gaze dropped another fifty degrees in temperature. "I wasn't trying to bribe you."

She gave him one of those teacher looks.

"Well, maybe I was, a little, but what's the big deal? A trip to McDonald's isn't like moving in together."

If her expression was anything to judge by, he'd gone from bad to worse.

Jacey tugged on her mother's hand. "Please, Mommy? John was really good today. We could say thank-you and pay for his hamburger. You always say we have to say thank-you when someone does something nice for us."

Once again, he was reminded of what a terrific mother Rachel was. When she turned to her daughter, all the anger and coldness had left her face. "You're right, Jacey. I forgot. We'll buy Mr. Crewes a hamburger to say thank-you."

John wondered if he'd only imagined that she'd added that they'd never see him again after his hamburger. It certainly seemed clear when she turned back to look at him.

"We'll worry about who pays when we get there. Step this way, ladies. My carriage awaits." He swept his arm toward his Porsche in a grand gesture.

"What's a carriage?" Jacey immediately asked, pushing past her mother and out the door.

"It's what Cinderella rode in to the ball," Rachel murmured and then added, "we'll take our car and meet you there."

"Don't be silly, Rachel." Another mistake, he realized as she turned to stare at him, one eyebrow rising in warning. He hurriedly added, "There's no reason to take two cars."

"You're right. You can ride with us."

He looked at the ancient car in her driveway and then the gleaming black Porsche he drove and swallowed. But he wasn't going to let her keep him from going with them. "Okay."

Jacey clapped her hands and ran to her mother's car. She slipped into the back seat and fastened her seat belt at once. John walked around the car and took the passenger seat, even though every instinct told him to offer to drive. He wasn't used to a woman driving him somewhere.

"Good girl, Jacey," he praised as he fastened his own seat belt.

"What did I do?" the child asked, her eyes wide.

"You fastened your seat belt."

"Mommy won't start the car until I do."

Rachel was settling in behind the wheel and ignoring them.

"Ah. Good mommy."

Jacey giggled and Rachel smiled at her daughter, but she didn't extend that warmth to him. So far, everything was normal.

When they reached McDonald's, all three stood in line together. Rachel pointedly gave the order for her and Jacey and pulled out her billfold to pay.

John looked at the teenage boy behind the cash register. "We're together." He added his order and handed over a twenty-dollar bill before Rachel realized what he was doing.

"No! We—"

"Don't be difficult, Rachel," he said and grinned at the boy. "Women!" he murmured and Rachel glared at him again. "You and Jacey go find us a place to sit."

Frustration flattened out her wonderfully full lips and she whirled around and walked away. He hoped she wouldn't keep walking until she reached her car.

He picked up the quickly loaded tray and scanned the restaurant. He'd gotten lucky. She and Jacey were sitting on one side of a booth for four people over by a window. He carried the tray over and slid in across from them.

"Okay, Jacey, my girl. Here's your Happy Meal."

He offered Rachel her choices also, before taking his own food off the tray.

Rachel didn't start eating, like Jacey did. Instead, she fixed a steady look on John. "Jacey said your speech went well this morning. But how did Mrs. Wilson react to your explanation about not being Jacey's daddy?"

He'd been right. Jacey hadn't explained.

He didn't want to, either.

Chapter Three

Rachel stared at the man across from her, waiting for an answer. When he looked at her daughter, she turned to Jacey also.

"Jacey?" she asked, noting her daughter's fearful expression.

"It really wasn't her fault," John hurriedly said. "I was late, so..." He trailed off, shrugging his shoulders.

"What wasn't Jacey's fault? Did you tell your teacher that Mr. Crewes was not your new daddy?" Rachel asked her child.

Jacey picked up a French Fry and slowly swirled it through a puddle of thick catsup. "Not 'zactly."

"Janet Cecilia Cason!" Rachel exclaimed.

"Mommy!" Jacey protested. She hated it when Rachel used all her names. It meant she was upset.

"I think you have some explaining to do, young lady."

"Now, wait a minute," John began, trying, she supposed, to save her daughter from a scolding. She glared at him, halting his interruption. She feared he could charm her into a lot of things, but her role as a parent was too important to give in to any persuading from him.

"I was going to, Mommy, but I waited for John to arrive, 'cause, well, 'cause he's so big, I wouldn't be afraid if he was with me, like a real daddy."

Soulful eyes looked first at John and then at Rachel. It didn't take a rocket scientist to see that John was completely taken in by Jacey's statement.

"Aw, Jacey, I'm sorry I was late," he said and extended his hand across the table to hold hers.

Rachel worked to keep a frown on her face as the pair of them turned their pleading eyes her way. "Oh, no. I'm not that gullible, Jacey. I told you to explain to Mrs. Wilson as soon as you got to school."

"She was busy, Mommy."

"And why didn't you explain when you got there, John Crewes, since you seem so willing to excuse Jacey for not setting the record straight?"

"Mrs. Wilson shoved me in front of the kids at once because I was late. Lisbeth's father had already finished. If I was going to confess, everyone in the room would've heard me. I didn't want to embarrass Jacey like that."

Rachel almost groaned aloud. It was hard enough to be strict with Jacey, even though she knew it was in Jacey's best interests, without someone else siding with her little girl. Squaring her jaw, she asked, "And afterward?"

"Reading circle," he explained gravely, then added, in a fairly close rendition of Mrs. Wilson's precise tones, "We wouldn't want to get off schedule, now, would we?"

She ignored Jacey's giggly appreciation of his talent. "It is not polite to mock Mrs. Wilson. She is a fine teacher."

He ducked his head and mumbled an apology in the manner of some of the senior boys she taught. With an exasperated sigh, she turned back to her daughter.

"Jacey, why didn't you explain afterward?"

"'Cause the van came for child care, Mommy. I was afraid they'd leave me behind."

Since Jacey had been left behind once because she dawdled over putting away her supplies, her mother had lectured her about being on time for the van.

"Come on, Rachel, it's not that big a deal," John assured her when she covered her eyes with one hand.

She quickly glared at him again. "Maybe not to you. But now my child's teacher thinks I'm married to a total stranger!"

"How often do you talk to the woman?"

Rachel drew a deep breath. Maybe John Crewes was right. She'd write a note tomorrow, explaining how the silly misunderstanding had occurred. And that would be that.

"Okay, I'll straighten it out tomorrow."

"Do we have to tell Mrs. Wilson?" Jacey asked in a small voice.

Rachel noted that Jacey, who loved a Happy Meal, had scarcely eaten anything. She hadn't meant to ruin her daughter's treat. "Yes, we do, sweetheart, but I'll do the explaining this time. Everything will be all right." She peered into Jacey's box. "Did you find your surprise in the Happy Meal?"

"No."

Jacey leaned against the back of the booth, a sorrowful look on her face.

"If you don't want it, I saw a little boy over there who didn't get a Happy Meal. Why don't you offer it to him so it won't go to waste."

Her ploy distracted Jacey from her thoughts as she scanned the restaurant searching for the little boy who might take her prize. "I think I'd like to keep it, Mommy."

"If you want." Rachel picked up her hamburger and took a bite, as if everything was A-okay. If she ignored the handsome man sitting across from her, maybe it was.

"What are you going to use to distract *me?*" he murmured to Rachel as Jacey turned her attention to the toy in the plastic bag.

"Why would I want to distract you?"

"I don't know. So I'll eat my hamburger?"

The twinkle in his hazel eyes invited her smile, but she put the brakes on even as the corners of her mouth began to turn up. "Frankly, Mr. Crewes, I don't care whether you ever eat again. You and your ridiculous response to Jacey have caused me all kinds of problems. Watching you starve to death might be quite enjoyable."

"I've said it before but I'll say it again. You are one tough lady, Rachel Cason."

"Yes, I am," she agreed, hoping her smile didn't reveal how much his teasing affected her; how tempting it was to relax and invite him to come closer. Instead, she vowed to avoid her neighbor from now on.

Life seemed so easy for John Crewes. A smile, a wink, and the world was his. Money didn't hurt either. According to her neighbors, he was loaded. Quite a difference from her own life, with its constant struggle to provide for herself and Jacey.

Yes, she should definitely avoid this man, if for no other reason than that his all-American good looks—from his sandy hair casually brushed back to his hazel eyes that could twinkle with such mischief—were too tempting. His broad shoulders and strong physique were the icing on the cake.

Ignoring John Crewes might take more strength than she had.

JOHN RAN A HAND through his hair in frustration. What was the matter with him? He couldn't concentrate this morning. Annual reports held no interest in comparison to Rachel. Her blue eyes, her full lips that she tried to keep firmly set, her enticing curves, all lured him away from business.

He might as well forget her, though. She'd made it clear last night that she wanted nothing more to do with him.

And she was right. What did they have in common? He was a businessman, dedicated to making money, for himself and others. She was a schoolteacher, sacrificing to bring knowledge to a bunch of unappreciative teenagers.

Besides, she was a mother.

Jacey. The name alone brought a smile to John's face. What a kid! She'd finally brightened up last evening and finished her Happy Meal. Then she'd invited John to join her on the playground. It was the best offer he got, so the two of them went off, hand in hand, leaving her mother at the table.

They'd had a great time, even though he'd kept an eye on Rachel, too. Just in case she needed him. There could be some bad guys lurking at McDonald's, just looking to hit on a beautiful woman all alone.

Yeah, sure.

He'd tried to make up with Rachel when they reached their respective houses. She'd listened to his apology and thanked him for his concern for Jacey.

Then she'd told him to get lost. Only in nicer words.

"Mr. Crewes?" His secretary's voice intruded into his thoughts through the intercom. "David Wester is on line two."

"Thanks," he calmly acknowledged, but surprise mixed with a mild panic filled him. What could the man want? Did he already know that John had lied yesterday?

"David, this is John. How can I help you?"

First David complimented him again on his magic show of the day before. Obviously he didn't know *yet* just how much magic John's appearance had involved.

"The real reason I'm calling, John, is because I'm in the market for a new financial adviser. After meeting you yesterday, I checked into your reputation, and I must say, I am very impressed."

John took a deep breath. His small company had grown over the past few years, with the occasional hiccup, or maybe a choke, like during his divorce. He certainly was earning a large sum of money each year. But David Wester's account would at least double his company's size.

"Thank you, David. We're doing all right."

"Better than all right. But I wouldn't consider your company based solely on the numbers. I was impressed with you yesterday because of your ability to relate to the children, in particular Jacey. You're the kind of man I want to work with. A family man, one who puts people above money."

John thanked David again, feeling guilty about the misrepresentation, but unsure exactly how to explain. "I'd certainly be willing to look at your investments and give you my opinion of what I could do for you."

"No," David replied and John was surprised at how much relief was mixed with the disappointment. "No, I've already made up my mind. I want you to take over my commodities investments at once."

"But, David, shouldn't we talk first? Let me tell you what I might have in mind?"

"No, John, that's not necessary. I make my decisions based on the person, not his performance record, though yours is excellent. I'm a psychologist, remember?"

"But—"

"Now, I want you to get together with Bud Cassidy, my vice president. He's putting together all the information you'll need and can answer any questions. I work more on the creative end of our business and I've got a new project going that I think you'll be interested in. But more about that later."

"But—"

"You *can* meet with Bud right away, can't you?"

"Of course, but—"

"Great. Now, Friday night, I want you to come to dinner at seven. And bring Jacey and your wife. Lisbeth and her mother are looking forward to visiting with them. Casual, of course. Okay?"

"David, I—"

"I have to go now, John. See you Friday."

Before John could say anything else, the line went dead.

Stunned, he hung up the phone and sat staring at the far wall. David Wester was turning some of his investments over to him. John had no fears about being able to do the job; he was good at what he did.

His only fear was that David had based his decision on a falsehood. What would happen when he found out the truth? And he was sure to find out. After all, Rachel had said she would straighten out the misunderstanding today.

After ten minutes of debating his options, John decided that honesty was essential. He called David Wester's office.

"Mr. Wester, please, John Crewes calling."

"I'm sorry, Mr. Crewes, but Mr. Wester is out of the office. May I take a message?"

"But I just talked to him a few minutes ago."

"Oh, he probably called you from his car phone. He was on his way to the airport."

"When will he be back?" He certainly couldn't make the explanation to a secretary.

"He'll be back in the office next Monday, but I believe he'll be back in town Friday afternoon, late. May I take a message, or could someone else help you?"

"Is Bud Cassidy in?"

"Mr. Cassidy is in a meeting. I'll ask him to return your call when he's available."

Frustrated, John hung up the phone. Great. Just great. The biggest challenge of his career, and he was going to lose it. Even worse, he was losing it because he'd broken one of his own rules. He believed in honesty. In fact, it was his constant honesty that had saved him when his wife had tried to destroy him. He and Jacey, between them, had broken that rule. Only she was just a little girl. *He* should have known better.

Maybe if he had a chance to explain to David before he heard the truth from Lisbeth, John might be able to convince him that his motives were pure, even if he had lied. But that wouldn't happen. David would hear it from Lisbeth if from no one else, when—

What if Lisbeth, or Mrs. Wilson, didn't find out about the lie until Monday? What if he could convince Rachel to put off her explanation?

Memory of her attitude last evening made such a possibility doubtful. Normally he would approve of a woman who believed in honesty above all else. It made a rare but pleasant change from his ex-wife. *Great, Crewes. You find a woman who insists on honesty just when you need a good lie.*

He grinned as he remembered Rachel's stubborn little chin. But she had a weakness. One that was swiftly becoming a weakness for him, too. Jacey. She might agree to help him because of Jacey. It was worth a try. If he could just have a little breathing room, until he could talk to David face-to-face, maybe—

He reached for the phone and then realized he didn't even know where Rachel taught, much less the number. The one person in his neighborhood he knew was Polly Meadows, an elderly widow. He seized the telephone directory to look for her number.

"Polly, this is John Crewes from across the street. I'm trying to get hold of Rachel Cason."

"Why, John, I didn't even know you knew each other. Every time I've offered to introduce Rachel to you, she always refused."

That was an irritating thought that he put away for another day. A less hectic day.

"Uh, Polly, I'm kind of in a hurry. Do you know where Rachel teaches school?"

"Why, yes, of course. She's at Daniel Webster High School. She teaches history."

"Thank you, Polly," he hurriedly said, before she could launch into a description of Rachel's day. The woman was kind but long-winded. He searched through the telephone directory again and dialed a second number.

"Webster High School."

"Rachel Cason, please," he said authoritatively.

"I'll be happy to take a message. Mrs. Cason is in class right now."

"When will she be out of class?"

"I'm not sure. I'll put a message in her box and she'll return your call at her convenience."

"But I need to talk to her right away."

"I'm sorry, but—"

"But it's an emergency! Surely you have a way of reaching your teachers in an emergency?" Frustration was building in him.

"Well, if it's really an emergency..." The stern voice paused, as if waiting for him to confess to a practical joke.

"Yes, it is!" Well, it was for him. And what could it hurt to interrupt a class for a few minutes?

"I'll send a student to her class with a message. What shall I say?"

"Ask her to call John Crewes at 555-8714 at once."

"And shall I say it's an emergency?"

The lady still doubted him.

"Yes!"

He slammed down the phone and waited. He'd had no idea teachers were so incommunicado. How did Rachel stand it? He felt lost if he didn't have a telephone beside him.

Fifteen minutes later, he was still waiting, frustration building in him. When his secretary finally announced Rachel's call, John clenched the receiver as if it were a lifeline.

"John? This is Rachel. What's the matter?"

"Why did it take you so long? I said it was an emergency!"

"John, I had twenty-six seniors in class. I couldn't just walk out and leave them to their own devices."

"What if Jacey had been sick? Does she have to wait until it's convenient?" he demanded, outrage filling him.

"Jacey? Is this call about Jacey?" The rising panic in her voice filled him with guilt.

"No. At least, not exactly."

"Hurry up, then, John. My next class starts in two minutes."

"Have you talked to Mrs. Wilson?" he demanded, although he wanted to protest at being limited to such a short call. But he couldn't afford to waste the time.

"I sent a note with Jacey this morning."

"Oh."

"What's the matter?"

"I was going to ask you to postpone telling her."

"What difference does it make when I tell her? I think it's better to do disagreeable tasks at once."

"You would," John muttered, the tension flowing out of him like air escaping from a punctured balloon.

"What? I couldn't hear you."

"Never mind. I'm sorry I disturbed you."

"John? What's wrong?"

He could hear a bell ring in the background and Rachel gasped. Afraid she would hang up, he hurriedly said, "I'll explain later. When we both have more time."

Before Rachel could ask again, he hung up the phone and sagged against the back of his chair.

"Mr. Crewes, Mr. Cassidy is on line one," his secretary announced.

John sighed and picked up the phone again, punching the appropriate button.

After a brief introduction, Bud Cassidy wanted to set up a meeting time for the next day.

"Look, Mr. Cassidy, I—"

"Make it Bud. We'll be working together a lot."

"Okay, Bud, I don't think— I mean, I can meet with you tomorrow, but I'm not sure David is going to want me to handle his account."

"He's already decided. David's that way, John. He makes fast decisions and is seldom wrong."

"I think in this instance—"

"Look, he's out of town for a few days. Why don't we hold some preliminary meetings and we'll go from there."

John gave up. It was like he was caught in the undertow in the ocean, powerless to change his direction. "Okay. How about tomorrow at ten? Shall I come to your office...? No, I'll be happy to have you come here. All-right. I'll see you then."

John hung up the phone and swiveled around in his chair to stare out the window of his office. What a mess! All because he couldn't resist a pair of big blue eyes. Make that two pairs of big blue eyes.

JACEY FINGERED THE piece of folded paper in her shirt pocket as she waited for class to begin. Her mother had told her exactly what she was supposed to do with it.

She had intended to follow her mother's directions.

She really had.

But Lisbeth had run up to her as soon as she arrived and started talking about the summer and the vacation her new daddy was going to give her—the three of them—at Walt Disney World. Then another little girl started talking about the family vacation she was going to take. Soon Mrs. Wilson was letting everyone tell of their plans.

Then she asked Jacey where her new daddy and her mommy were going to take her, and she said Disney World, too, because she wanted everyone to think that her new daddy was just as wonderful as Lisbeth's.

"Let's go together!" Lisbeth squealed. "It would be just like we're sisters!"

"Yeah, sisters!" Jacey exclaimed eagerly, but already she was discovering the truth of her mother's warning. Lies always got you in trouble. She might be able to pretend that John was her daddy, but she knew he wasn't going to take her to Disney World just because she wanted him to.

That was why she was fingering the note in her pocket. She should give it to Mrs. Wilson at once. Like her mommy had told her to. But Mrs. Wilson would make her apologize to the class, like she did Peter last week when he said a bad word. On the playground afterward, everyone had laughed at him.

"All right, class, it's time to practice our counting."

Too late. Mrs. Wilson was starting class.

Jacey would give it to her later. Maybe at the end of school, before the van came. Maybe.

Jacey watched for the right moment, not wanting to fail her mother, but not wanting to be laughed at and teased by the other students. Finally, when the bell rang, she took her courage in her hands and approached Mrs. Wilson's desk.

"Come along, child. You don't want to miss the van again," Mrs. Wilson encouraged as the last of the others went through the door.

Jacey opened her mouth to explain why she'd waited, but the appearance of the principal at the door with another child and two adults halted her.

"Jacey, run along, child," Mrs. Wilson insisted as she greeted the new student and her parents.

With a shrug of her shoulders, Jacey ran along.

But she wasn't sure how she was going to explain to her mother that, once again, she had failed to keep her promise.

Chapter Four

Rachel picked Jacey up from child care without her usual smile. Nor did she ask any questions about Mrs. Wilson's reaction to the note.

"Are you okay, Mommy?" Jacey asked after riding in silence almost all the way home.

"What?" Rachel looked at Jacey as if she was surprised to see her there. "Oh, sorry, honey, what did you say?"

"Are you okay? You're not talking."

"I'm fine. I—I just had a hard day at school, baby. One of my students was upset."

Uh-oh, Jacey thought. If her mommy was already unhappy, the fact that she hadn't given the note to Mrs. Wilson wasn't going to cheer her up. Jacey slid down as far as the seat belt would allow and closed her eyes, as if she, too, had had a bad day.

The two rode in silence until Rachel turned into the driveway. Jacey opened her eyes and looked at John's house. She saw his car in the driveway and then noticed him standing inside by the big window at the front of his house. Funny, before she'd asked him to be her daddy when she needed one, she never remembered seeing his car at home.

"Look, Mommy, there's John," she said as she opened the car door and scooted out, waving.

"Come inside, Jacey," her mother said, and her tone wasn't friendly.

"Don't you like John, Mommy?"

"Jacey—"

"Hello!"

Both Jacey and her mother turned to see John striding across his yard and driveway to greet them.

"Hello," Rachel said in return, but she didn't smile.

"I thought I'd explain about the phone call," John said.

"What phone call?" Jacey asked. She smiled as John's hand came to rest on her head, just like a real daddy's.

He squatted down beside her and grinned. "I called your mom at school today. How did your day go? Was it rough?"

She knew what he was asking, and that was the one question she didn't want to answer. "Uh, not as bad as Mommy's."

His eyebrows almost came together and he looked all worried like the daddies on television when something was the matter with their family. She liked it.

"Rachel, my phone call wasn't what made your day so bad, was it?" John asked.

"No, of course not. Just forget it," she said and abruptly turned away to walk toward the house.

Jacey and John exchanged looks before they both followed Rachel. When they got to the door, Rachel had already entered the house.

"May I come in?" John called as he paused at the door.

"Yes, if you must," Rachel answered.

John knelt down beside Jacey again. "Maybe you'd better let me talk to your mom alone, Jacey."

"Okay," she agreed and hugged his neck. Sometimes, when her mommy was sad, like today, she wanted to make her happy, but she didn't know how. It was nice to have someone else to take care of her mommy.

And besides, it meant she didn't have to tell her mommy she hadn't given Mrs. Wilson the note—just yet.

"I'll go upstairs," she whispered and ran to her room.

"WHAT WENT WRONG today?"

Rachel spun around, her hand at her throat. An inquisition by John Crewes was the last thing she needed. It had been one of those days when everything went wrong. She'd ruined her nylons on the rough wood of her old desk and been run over by one of the football players making a mad dash to practice. Then she'd found out about Diane. "Look, John, what do you want? I don't have time—"

"I was just concerned, Rachel. Can't I be concerned? You look like you lost your best friend."

There was a warmth in his voice that was incredibly tempting. Rachel had stood alone for so many years without the luxury of a shoulder to cry on, figuratively or otherwise. She looked at him, trying to imagine resting against his lean body.

Then she didn't have to imagine anymore. He took a step closer and pulled her into his arms, offering her his shoulder. She was too stunned, too tempted, to say no. He felt so heavenly, so strong, so . . . so male.

Contrary to her earlier thoughts, crying wasn't what came to mind as she rested against him. Feelings she'd thought buried long ago were tunneling through her, seeking life. No! she silently protested. She didn't need a man—any man.

With more strength than she realized, she pushed him away and turned her back on him.

"I'm fine. What did you need?"

He circled around her. "Why are you blushing?"

"Don't be silly. It's just the afternoon heat." And the nearness of John Crewes. He'd changed out of his business suit and into cutoffs and a polo shirt. Except for his broad shoulders and a few laugh wrinkles at the corners of his eyes, he looked more like a college kid than a businessman.

He sighed and she peeped at him from under her lashes. She wished he'd quit staring at her.

"Okay, I just wondered how things went with Mrs. Wilson. You know, if Jacey had a hard time when you explained to the woman."

"Oh, dear," Rachel muttered. "I forgot all about it."

"You mean you didn't tell her?"

There was an eagerness in his voice that reminded her of his phone call. "Wait a minute. That's the reason you called, isn't it? You wanted me to wait. Why?"

He shrugged his shoulders and his face had that sheepish look that Jacey wore when she'd been caught doing something she shouldn't.

"I got a call from David Wester today," he said, as if that would explain everything.

Rachel vaguely recognized the name but it didn't mean anything to her. Probably someone big in the business world. She shrugged. "So?"

"You don't know who he is?"

"No, sorry."

"He's Lisbeth's new daddy."

Ah. Now she caught the significance. "The other daddy who came to show-and-tell?"

"That's right. He spoke to the class before I arrived." John ran his hand through his thick, sandy hair and Rachel looked away hurriedly. She was far too tempted to do the same thing.

To put some distance between the two of them, she walked around the couch and sat down in the rocking chair she'd had since Jacey was born.

"Rachel, are you paying attention?" John asked, following her.

She pressed against the back of the rocker as he leaned toward her. Her breathing speeded up as she fought the urge to feel his arm around her again. "Of course, I am. What's the point to the story?"

"Do you know what David Wester does?"

"John, why should I care what he does?" she asked in frustration. "It's been a long day. I'm tired and hungry, I have a five-year-old to feed, and a stack of papers to grade." *And you're too hard on my nervous system.*

Silence reigned and Rachel finally opened her eyes to find John staring at her. "Look, I'm sorry. I know that was impolite, but—"

"But you need a little space."

She was surprised to discover that he understood how she was feeling, and even more surprised to discover how desperately she needed some time to herself. "Yes," she agreed with a big sigh.

"Okay. I'll take Jacey to get some dinner for us. Chinese okay? We won't hurry. You put your feet up and relax."

"No! You can't do that. You bought dinner last night." She wasn't turning her life over to this man. She'd just met him Saturday.

John ignored her protest and walked over to the foot of the stairs. "Jacey!" he called.

Getting up from the rocker, Rachel followed him, prepared to protest again. Her daughter appeared at the head of the stairs.

"Let's go get some Chinese food for dinner while your mom rests, okay?"

"Oh, boy, can I have sweet-and-sour chicken?" Jacey asked as she rushed down the stairs. "I love that, and baby corn, and fortune cookies!"

"You can have all of it, sweetheart."

"And can we stop off at the park and feed the ducks?" Jacey added.

"Sounds good to me," John agreed.

Rachel protested, but the two of them were ignoring her and making plans faster than she could even think. "John, don't—" she tried again.

"We'll be back in about an hour, Rachel," John calmly said, taking Jacey's hand. Then he startled Rachel by leaning over and kissing her cheek, casually, as if it were a common thing.

Before she could pull herself together, the two of them were out the door, smiles on their faces.

Rachel stared after them, her mouth hanging open. He'd acted just like a husband. A real husband, who understood that his wife needed his care as much as his child did, sometimes. A husband of her dreams.

Get real, Cason! She mustn't let this temporary intrusion into her life upset her. Or mislead her into thinking anything was going to be different.

He wasn't her husband. He wasn't Jacey's daddy. And he wasn't going to remain in their lives.

JOHN AND JACEY STOPPED at a drive-in grocery and bought a loaf of bread and some canned sodas before they went to the park. The big white ducks were bold when they discovered the little girl had food.

Jacey shrieked and giggled, chasing and being chased, for more than half an hour. John hovered in the background, anxious to protect her but not wanting to spoil her fun.

Finally, he called her over to a picnic bench and offered her a cold soda. "You should be about ready for this," he said with a grin.

"Do we have some for the ducks?"

"Jacey, you can't give ducks soda. They drink water from the pond."

"Ooh, but it smells. And Mommy says I can't drink the water in the swimming pool."

He gently tweaked her button nose. "That's because you're not a duck."

"Okay. I'm having fun. Thank you."

"You're welcome. You have very nice manners."

"My mommy taught me."

"You have a very nice mommy, too."

"I know," Jacey agreed with a giggle.

"Does she come home upset often?"

"No. Only when a kid at school makes her sad," Jacey said, her gaze on the ducks.

"How do they make her sad? Do they do bad things?"

"No, Mommy makes them behave. But sometimes they don't have anyone to love them, and that makes her sad."

"I see," John said. And he did. Rachel Cason had a big heart. He knew her child never doubted for a minute that her mother loved her. He'd seen it in the way she dealt with Jacey. Even when Jacey had misbehaved, Rachel showed her love.

John's father had been busy with his job. His mother had had her charity work. And he had been left alone, with rules to follow and chores to do. He hadn't suffered. Affluent parents were an asset he didn't discount. But the idea of having a mother like Rachel, giving her child a hug, a smile, her time—ah, that would have been heaven.

Of course, a hug from Rachel now might be even better. He chuckled, thinking about her reaction to his thoughts.

"What's so funny?" Jacey asked, tugging on his shirt.

"I was just thinking about how nice your mom is."

"Yeah," Jacey replied in a satisfied voice.

"Where's your daddy?" The question slipped out before John thought about the implications for Jacey. He wished he could take it back, but he discovered the child was quite at ease.

"He left before I was borned. Mommy says he didn't know I was going to be this good, or he wouldn't have left."

He hugged her to him. "I'm sure your mommy is right, 'cause you're one special kid, Jacey."

"You're a good daddy, too," Jacey said, smiling up at him. "I picked a good daddy to hire."

"I don't have any experience."

"Mommy didn't have no experience to be a mommy, neither. She said she was scared. But she learned real fast."

"She certainly did. Let's go get some Chinese food and go back home. Maybe she's feeling better by now."

He hoped so. When she looked at him with those forlorn blue eyes, all he wanted to do was to take her into his arms and comfort her. He didn't think Rachel would react well to such an offer. But he couldn't help thinking about what Jacey had said. Her daddy had left before she was born.

Who had stood by Rachel? Her parents? Jacey hadn't mentioned grandparents. It seemed to him, if she had a grandfather, she would have asked *him* to do show-and-tell.

Did that mean Rachel had been all alone, pregnant? How old was she when Jacey was born?

His mind occupied with all the questions he wanted to ask Rachel, John didn't think of his original question until they'd gone through the drive-through at the Chinese restaurant and were almost back home.

"Say, Jacey, what did Mrs. Wilson say when she found out I'm not really your dad?"

The smile that had been on Jacey's face the entire trip abruptly disappeared.

"Was it bad, sweetheart?" John asked, his heart going out to Jacey. "I'm sorry."

Jacey's chin dropped down to her chest and she muttered something. John frowned, but he couldn't take his eyes off the road long enough to comfort her. That teacher must have been brutal.

He pulled into the driveway and killed the motor, then turned to Jacey. "Come on, sweetheart, tell me what she said."

"I can't," Jacey whispered.

"She can't have been that mean, Jacey. Did she make you tell the class?"

She shook her head no.

A thought struck him and he looked at Jacey in horror. "She didn't spank you, did she?"

"No."

"Jacey, talk to me. Did she chew you out?"

The child shook her head again.

Frustration built in him. As cute as he thought Jacey was, John wanted an answer. He was beginning to understand why parents lost their tempers with children.

"Jacey?"

"I didn't give her the note." Jacey kept her gaze focused on her toes.

Prepared to comfort her for the horrible punishment she'd received, John needed a moment to understand what she'd said.

"What? She doesn't know?"

Jacey shook her head.

"Did you tell Lisbeth?" he asked, checking all his bases.

Jacey shook her head a second time. Then, looking at John briefly before turning her gaze down again, she added, in a rush, "Lisbeth's going to Disney World with her new daddy."

John had no interest in Lisbeth's activities. He was busy thinking about the significance of Jacey's answer. "Okay," he said absently.

"I said we were, too."

"Fine. Sweetheart, have you told your mother that you didn't give her note to Mrs. Wilson?"

"No." They sat in silence. Then Jacey asked in a small voice, "You aren't mad?"

John laughed out loud. "Mad? No, I'm pleased." Then he thought about the message that might give a small child. "But I'm not your mother. She's not going to be happy that you didn't obey her, you know."

"I know."

"When are you going to tell her?"

"I could just give Mrs. Wilson the note tomorrow."

"No!" John hadn't meant to snap his reply. "No, I mean, I don't think that's a good idea."

"Why not?"

"Because—because I think you should tell your mommy tonight."

"But then she'll be upset, and she's already sad."

Jacey was right. And if he didn't need to discuss with Rachel the idea of not telling Mrs. Wilson until Monday, it would have been a perfect answer. Jacey wouldn't get in trouble and Rachel wouldn't be unhappy.

He felt like a rat.

Because of his needs, Jacey was going to have to confess to her mother that she hadn't given the note to Mrs. Wilson.

"Sweetheart, I—"

Tapping on his car window scared both of them.

He discovered Rachel bending over, looking in at them. The view of her blouse gaping just a little, revealing shadowy mounds of flesh that would figure in future dreams, was almost worth the interruption. As he brought his gaze back to her face, she grabbed her blouse and straightened, her cheeks red.

Jacey opened her car door.

"We had fun, Mommy. We fed the ducks lots of bread."

"Good. You were gone a long time."

John got out of the car, juggling the cartons of Chinese food and the extra sodas in a grocery sack.

"Hungry?" he asked, his gaze searching her face.

"Yes, starving, but I feel bad about your going to so much trouble."

"No trouble. We had fun, like Jacey said."

Which was more than they were going to have now, John thought to himself as he followed Jacey and her mother into the house.

Maybe he'd wait to bring up the subject of Mrs. Wilson and the note until after dinner. No point in ruining everyone's meal.

Chapter Five

Rachel studied John out of the corner of her eye as he talked to Jacey. What a surprise the evening had been.

First, he'd understood her need for solitude. Not only understood, but also done something about providing it. Then, he'd brought home a delicious dinner and proceeded to share it with them.

And entertained them.

He'd told funny stories that even she couldn't resist. Jacey had giggled all evening long. Now she was curled up in John's lap, helping him read his fortune from the broken fortune cookie on his plate.

"'You will have health, wealth and happiness,'" John read, pointing to each word for Jacey's benefit.

"Is that good?" the little girl asked, hoping, Rachel decided, that John would only get good news.

"The best," he assured her and kissed the top of her head.

Rachel wanted to protest. Her child was growing too fond of this man. And they'd only known him less than a week. Jacey would be terribly upset when John bowed out of their lives.

"What does mine say?" Jacey asked, pulling the thin strip of paper from her fortune cookie.

John took the paper from her and then laughed as he silently read it.

"What does it say? What does it say?" Jacey asked anxiously.

"It says, 'It is wise to listen to your elders.'" His gaze lifted from the paper to meet Rachel's, inviting her to laugh with him.

The best she could muster was a smile.

"What's an elder?" Jacey wanted to know.

"Your mom and me," he said.

"An elder is someone who is older than you, Jacey. Usually much older," Rachel added.

Jacey didn't seem as amused as John. She looked up at him and then at her mother. "Okay," she said with a sigh and began to slide down from John's lap.

"Jacey? Where are you going?" he asked.

Rather than answer him, Jacey came around the table and stood in front of her mother. "I have to tell you something, Mommy. John said I should."

Rachel glanced at John and then Jacey. Before either she or Jacey could speak, however, John stood.

"No, Jacey. I was wrong. Do it your way."

Jacey's finger stole to her mouth, as it always did when she was worried or scared. Rachel cupped her stubborn little chin in one hand.

"What is it, Jacey?"

Her daughter looked back at John. "No, you were right, John. Mommy, I didn't give the note to Mrs. Wilson today."

Rachel closed her eyes briefly and then looked at Jacey. "Why not, sweetie?"

"Because I was afraid she would make me apologize to the class, like she did Peter. Everybody laughed at him.'' Tears welled up in her big blue eyes. ''I'm sorry, Mommy. Are you mad at me?''

Rachel wrapped her arms around her daughter and held her. ''No, I'm not mad. I'm a little disappointed that you didn't do what I asked, but maybe I expected too much.''

''I'll give it to her tomorrow, Mommy, I promise!'' Jacey exclaimed, her little arms encircling her mother's neck and hugging tightly.

''We'll see, Jacey. I'll think about what I want to do.'' Rachel hugged her again. ''Now, thank Mr. Crewes for our dinner and go get ready for bed.''

Jacey did more than thank John. She threw herself into his arms.

''May I give her a ride up the stairs?'' he asked as he picked Jacey up, swinging her to his shoulders.

The move had surprised a chuckle from Jacey and she grabbed his ears to hold on. How could Rachel say no when in one move he'd brought a smile back to Jacey's face?

''Yes, of course.'' Rachel stood back for him to pass in front of her and then followed the two of them up the stairs.

John deposited Jacey on her bed and told her goodnight. Rachel tried to thank him for their dinner, in case he wanted to leave while she was helping Jacey into bed, but he assured her he'd wait downstairs for her.

She didn't want him to wait. She didn't want to be alone with him, without Jacey's distracting presence. She didn't want to be tempted by his sexy body, his warmth, the sense of caring he'd dispensed that evening. She knew better than to believe such things would last.

He ignored her protests and went down the stairs.

"I love John," Jacey announced, as Rachel pulled her pajama top over her head.

"Jacey, John is very nice, but—but he's not a daddy, you know. Yours or anyone else's. He won't be coming here after tonight."

"Why not? He lives next door, Mommy. It's not a long way."

"I know it's not, sweetie, but men who aren't married, who don't have children, have lots of other things to do. They're too busy to play with little children." *Or single mothers.*

"Oh."

"Thank you for being honest about the note."

"I'm sorry I didn't give it to her."

"That's all right. Let's say your prayers now."

She listened as Jacey recited the prayer she used each evening. After the memorized words, Jacey always added her own special prayers, and Rachel cringed as her child talked.

"Thank you, God, for John. Let him come back to play with us. I'm sorry I didn't mind my mommy. Love, Jacey."

Rachel thought it was time to tuck her in, but Jacey had one more plea.

"And P.S., please make John be my daddy for real. Amen."

"Jacey!"

"What, Mommy? You said I could ask God for whatever I wanted."

"Yes, but—but he may not give you what you ask for. Remember?"

"I remember. But I thought I should ask."

"Good night, Jacey," Rachel whispered, kissing her daughter. She didn't want to discuss Jacey's request.

He might be the answer to her daughter's prayers, but John Crewes was a temptation she intended to avoid.

JOHN PACED THE FLOOR as he waited for Rachel in the comfortable living room. Earlier, he'd distracted himself by silently admiring Rachel's skill at taking old worn-out furniture and making it look comfortable and welcoming. Clearly, she and Jacey didn't have a lot, but she'd made a nice home for the two of them. Those thoughts didn't distract him now, however.

What mattered was convincing Rachel to wait until Monday before she told the truth to Mrs. Wilson.

"Thank you for telling Jacey to confess," Rachel said as she entered the room.

John's head snapped up and he stared at the beautiful woman before him.

"I can't take credit for that."

"Why not? She said she told me because you said it was the thing to do."

Her blue eyes were as large as Jacey's and even more delicious . . . along with the rest of her. He took a step closer and then stopped.

"When I said she should tell you, I was thinking about myself. After I thought about it, I decided it would be wrong to get Jacey into trouble just to help me."

Rachel's eyebrows rose as the warmth in her eyes faded. John knew exactly how a student might feel if he was guilty of breaking one of her rules.

"How would getting Jacey into trouble help you?"

"I needed to talk to you about telling Mrs. Wilson the truth. I couldn't do that if you thought Mrs. Wilson already knew."

She continued to pin him in his place with her stare as she crossed her arms. "This has to do with the phone call you made to me, doesn't it?"

He nodded.

"John, Mrs. Wilson must be informed of the truth. Otherwise, she'll change all Jacey's records, everything. I can't let this lie continue."

"I'm not suggesting you do," he assured her, taking another step closer. He wanted to run his hands up her arms, warm them into relaxation, cuddle her against him. He wanted to, but he wouldn't. At least not yet.

"Then just what are you suggesting?"

He gestured toward the couch. "Come sit down and let me explain. It might get a little complicated and there's no need to be uncomfortable."

Even though she moved toward the couch, she cast a suspicious eye on him. "The last man who wanted me to sit down and get comfortable was trying to sell me a set of encyclopedias. What are you trying to sell, John?"

"Nothing so expensive, I promise you." He was amused, however. He could think of a lot of things he'd want her to relax for. None of them involved encyclopedias.

Once seated a discreet distance from her on the couch, John tried to decide how best to explain his dilemma.

"Well?"

He gave her a sideways smile and plunged in. "David Wester called today to offer me his business because I'm such a family-oriented man."

"What? But that's not true!"

"I know."

"You did tell him, didn't you?" She was giving him her teacher look again.

"I tried, Rachel, but he was in a hurry, and he surprised me."

"John, I won't be a part of any lie, no matter how much money it would bring you."

"I'm not asking you to," he hastily assured her.

"It sounds like you are."

"That's because you haven't let me explain." He reached out and took her hand, surprised at how much he yearned just to touch her. The electric spark that flashed between them must have been obvious to her, too, because she pulled her hand away at once.

"I'm waiting," she assured him, but she wouldn't look at him. Her gaze was fixed on her hands, clasped in her lap, out of his reach.

"After David hung up, I thought about it for a few minutes. I'll admit," he said in response to her derisive look, "I thought about keeping quiet. But that's not how I do business. So I called him back to tell him the truth."

"Good."

"But he wasn't there. He'd called me on the way to the airport. He'll be out of town until Friday evening."

"Then it doesn't matter if I tell Mrs. Wilson tomorrow. He won't hear the news until he returns." Rachel gave a satisfied nod, as if she thought the matter had been settled.

"That's not true, Rachel. If Mrs. Wilson tells the class, Lisbeth will tell her mother and Mrs. Wester will tell her husband when she talks to him."

"But if you're going to tell him the truth anyway—"

"I am, I promise," he assured her, since he heard some doubt in her words. "But *I'd* like to be the one to tell him—not a five-year-old, or her mother."

"I don't see why—"

"Rachel, I was married once."

She stared at him blankly, not understanding his change of subject. He wished he didn't have to make this explanation, but Rachel needed to understand his situation.

"My wife was not happy with our marriage. She decided to divorce me, and she wanted to be sure she didn't have to work, so she tried to take me for everything I was worth. She lied and cheated and spread rumors that almost destroyed me. My good name is my most important asset. I almost lost it."

Rachel stared at him, her eyes round with astonishment.

"It is important to me that I be honest with David Wester. Whether he gives me his business or not, I must maintain my reputation for honesty and trustworthiness."

Her clasped hands tightened and she stared straight ahead, but she didn't say anything. He hadn't convinced her yet. Time for the heavy guns.

"I'm not asking you to lie to anyone. I'm just asking for a little time so I can explain everything to David myself, face-to-face. Then, if he doesn't want to give me his business, I won't complain."

Still no response.

"Is that so much to ask? After all, I was just trying to help out your little girl," he reminded, his eyes rounded in innocence. He hated to use Jacey, but it was the truth.

"John Crewes! I was against the idea in the first place, and Jacey is just a little girl! How dare you blame it on us!" She jumped to her feet and glared at him, her hands on her hips.

He rose to stand beside her, grinning. He loved to see Rachel all agitated, her bosom rising and falling in enticing rhythm. Besides, when she was upset, she forgot to keep him at a distance. "I'm not blaming Jacey. It's not her fault she doesn't have a daddy."

The heat faded from her, was replaced by a glacial look. "Please leave, Mr. Crewes." She turned her back, crossing her arms over her chest.

"Rachel," he said, "I helped Jacey. I'm only asking for a little help in return."

She whirled around, her eyes shooting darts of anger. "So far you have used my child against me, and then you had the gall to blame me for not hanging on to a man who wanted nothing to do with me or his baby. And you think *I* owe *you?*" She advanced toward him, pointing her finger at him.

John backed away, hoping to avoid an out-and-out fight. "Now, Rachel, let's be rational."

When his back hit the paneled wall, he decided it was time to take the offensive. Overwrought, Rachel didn't seem to realize he'd run out of territory. She was practically stomping on his toes when he grabbed her shoulders and pulled her into his arms. His lips seized her full, soft ones, halting her words.

He'd dreamed of tasting her lips, of mingling their breaths, of feeling her against him. He'd had no idea how glorious it would be, better than his dreams. Rachel didn't fight him. At first, he could feel the shock run through her body. Then there was a lightning flash of recognition, as there had been when he'd held her earlier. She sank against him, her lips opening to him, her arms stealing up around his neck.

Heaven.

What he'd started as a way of controlling Rachel was quickly turning into an uncontrollable riot for John. While his lips caressed hers, his hands slid to her waist, tugging at her blouse. *Forget David Wester. Forget Mrs. Wilson. Forget the world.* As his fingers caressed warm skin, he was lost to everything but Rachel.

As quickly as she'd given in, Rachel suddenly jerked away from his hold. "What do you think you're doing?" she demanded, her voice high with tension.

"The same thing you were doing," he assured her. "We were kissing, Rachel, and it felt damn good."

She crossed to the other side of the room. "Go away!"

"That's your response to everything that's happened? Go away?"

"Yes!"

"That doesn't sound very mature," he said, drawling his words with sarcasm. He'd really blown it. He feared Rachel wouldn't even talk to him after that kiss.

Something he'd said affected her. She drew several deep breaths before she spoke again. "You're right. I'm overreacting." Much to his surprise, she moved around the room, always keeping her distance from him, but didn't repeat her order for him to leave.

Finally she turned to face him, although her gaze went somewhere over his shoulder. "I will promise to wait until Monday to straighten out the—the situation with Mrs. Wilson, if you will promise to stay away from Jacey.''

Her request electrified him, as if he'd burned himself. ''What do you mean? Why can't I see Jacey?''

She looked him in the eye this time. ''Because she's already beginning to care for you. I don't want her hurt.''

''I care for her, too.''

Rachel rolled her eyes and turned away.

''What's that supposed to mean?'' He hurried around the end of the sofa to cut off her escape.

''I didn't say anything,'' she retorted, her chin in the air.

''You said something, all right. With your eyes, like you didn't believe me. Jacey is a sweetheart. I'd have to be made of stone not to care about her.''

He reached for her shoulders, wanting to make his point physically, and also wanting to touch her again. Just for a minute. Or longer, if she didn't protest.

She backed away.

''You may think you care about her, but something else will come along to distract you. You'll pursue it, and Jacey will be left crying because you didn't keep your promise.'' Her words were laced with bitterness, and he remembered Jacey's words about her father.

''I'm not Jacey's father.''

''Exactly my point,'' she agreed vehemently.

''No, Rachel. I'm saying I'm not like Jacey's real father.''

Her eyes widened and there was a vulnerability there that grabbed his heart. Before he could reach for her, however, she recovered.

"This is a pointless discussion, John Crewes. I'll keep the secret until Monday, but I don't want to see you over here again." Suddenly she was the poised teacher, staring down a difficult child.

John took a deep breath. Clearly, she wasn't going to continue their discussion. He should be grateful that step one was accomplished. But now, it was time for step two.

"Uh, thanks, Rachel. There's just one little problem."

"Only one? Are you sure? You seem to be full of problems." She was glaring at him again.

"Yeah. Only one. David invited the three of us to his house Friday night, and I was kind of counting on you and Jacey going with me."

He ducked as she picked up a big book and drew it back over her head.

Chapter Six

Rachel gasped as she saw John duck. His action brought home to her what she'd been about to do. Feeling decidedly silly, she lowered the book from over her head and carefully placed it back on the table.

"Rachel? I know that was a bit unexpected, but if you'll let me explain—"

"That's what you said about keeping the truth a secret for a few more days." The man was dangerous, no question about it. Dangerous because he appeared to be able to talk her into anything. Dangerous because he evoked an out-of-control reaction that frightened her. Dangerous because she was attracted to him.

"Just give me a couple of minutes."

She nodded, unwilling to trust herself to say anything. How did he do it? She'd been around attractive men before. She'd even tried dating a little after Jacey became a toddler. That was when she'd discovered that single men didn't want anything to do with a single mother.

She hadn't been heartbroken. No, she'd accepted the fact that having Jacey in her life eliminated certain things. And considered her child well worth the sacrifice.

Now her heart, her body, were sending messages to her brain that she'd thought didn't exist anymore. They'd picked an inconvenient time to emerge from a deep sleep.

"Rachel?"

"Very well. Explain."

"I don't suppose you'd consider getting comfortable again?" he suggested with a smile that would charm the birds from the trees, as he gestured toward the couch.

"I think not," she murmured and looked away. She didn't intend to get within touching distance of him ever again. She had to root these feelings out of herself.

"Look, Rachel, David extended the invitation with all the authority of a general ordering his troops. Now his wife is planning on having the three of us to dinner. If I'm the only one who shows up Friday night, we'll be starting the evening off on a bad note."

She gave him an exasperated look, hoping he'd understand how little that argument accomplished, although she admitted to herself that he was right.

"If the three of us go, you and I can explain to David and his wife about the mistake. If the two of us can laugh about it, I think it will minimize the damage. Then I can tell David that he's still free to make a choice about hiring me. And Jacey can spend the evening with Lisbeth."

"You don't honestly expect me to believe that you made these plans to provide Jacey an evening with Lisbeth, do you?" she asked, shaking her head.

"Of course not. *I* didn't plan any of this. All I wanted to do was help Jacey feel good about herself," he reminded her with a little testiness.

He was right, of course. His intentions had been good, even if the result was turning into an unending nightmare. And he'd done it for Jacey.

Rachel had promised herself long ago that she would be independent, relying on no one, owing no one. But she owed John Crewes for doing something special for her child.

Abruptly she asked, "What time Friday night?"

John stared, then moved toward her, a warm light in his eyes.

She put up a hand in defense and moved away from him. "Don't come near me."

"Why? I just wanted to say thank-you. At least, I assume your question meant you'll help me."

"Yes, I will, but I don't need you to thank me."

"But it would be so much fun, Rachel," he teased, seemingly lighthearted now that she'd agreed.

"John, I'm willing to go along with you because I don't think it will hurt anything and because you've been very kind to Jacey. But that's it. I'm not going to sleep with you."

Her words stopped him in his tracks. "Well, Rachel, I don't believe I asked for such a sacrifice."

With a grim smile, she said, "Yes, you did, John. Not in words, but with those hot looks you've been giving me. With your touching, with that kiss. I may not date right now, but I know men. How do you think I got Jacey?"

"From under a lettuce leaf?" he teased and took another step toward her.

"John!" she warned, moving away again.

He held up both hands in surrender, although, of course, she wasn't foolish enough to believe it.

"All right. I admit I'm attracted to you. You felt it, too, didn't you, Rachel? And I wouldn't complain if you stripped naked right this minute and lured me upstairs. No red-blooded male would, because you're a beautiful woman. But that's not what our agreement is about."

"No, it's not or I wouldn't have agreed," she assured him, keeping her voice cool even as her thoughts were turned to the word picture he'd created—only she thought about him stripping naked, not her. Ouch! Time to think of other things.

"Your cheeks are red again," he murmured, his gaze trained on her face.

And she knew why. His casual clothes couldn't hide the strength and breadth of his shoulders, his flat stomach, muscular legs. But even more tempting was the warmth in his eyes when he smiled at her child, the consideration he'd shown Rachel, and the silent offer to shield the two of them from the harshness of reality.

He was playing the role of knight in shining armor.

It was incredibly seductive.

And completely unbelievable.

After all, she'd been down that road once. It was a dead end. The only person she could trust was herself.

"It must be the heat," she said with a shrug.

"Yeah. I've felt the same heat. Are you sure you want to ignore it?"

"Absolutely." Before he could offer further arguments—and she could see he intended to—she repeated her earlier question: "You never said what time Friday night."

"Seven."

She nodded and began walking toward the door.

"We should probably leave here about a quarter 'til."

She nodded again, keeping her back to him.

"And this time I'll drive."

She turned to face him. "I could take my car, too. Then, after the explanation, Jacey and I could leave and you could have your business discussion."

"Rachel, we're not going to walk in the front door, spill our guts and turn around and walk out. We've been invited to dinner."

"Spilling their guts," as John had phrased it, seemed a lot easier than sitting down to dinner with people she'd lied to. "I don't think—" she began, only to discover she'd trapped herself against the front door, with John cutting off any hope of escape.

With a gentleness that was sexier than any bare chest she'd ever seen, he grasped her shoulders and smiled at her. "It will be all right, Rachel. Don't worry about it."

As if she could dismiss her worries—all one million of them. And most of them were centered on John Crewes.

"By the way," he suddenly said, "you never said what had upset you earlier."

She shrugged her shoulders. It was hard to switch gears so abruptly from the roles of mother and woman to that of teacher. Besides, she didn't want to confide in him. Did she?

"Jacey said you're sad sometimes because some of your students have problems."

She shrugged again, but this time his gaze caught hers. Finally, she muttered, "One of my students attempted suicide."

"Is he all right?"

"She's all right . . . for now."

"Do you know why?" His furrowed brow gave him the appearance of concern.

"Her boyfriend dumped her."

He stared at her for several seconds. Then he said, "Rachel, not all men are bastards. And she has to take responsibility for her decisions."

"Thank you, Doctor."

Much to her surprise, he grinned at her sarcastic response. "Okay, okay. I know it's not that simple. And I'm sorry, for her and for you."

"Why me?" she demanded, fearful that he'd read her mind, or knew of her past history.

"Because it upset you. Jacey and I don't like it when you're upset." That heart-stopping grin filled his face and her heart flipped over. Then it almost stopped beating as his gaze grew more serious and the grin changed to a startled look.

"Don't concern yourself with me," she hurriedly said, afraid of what he might say next. "You've got enough problems to deal with."

"You're right," he agreed with a sigh. "I'm going now. I just want you to know that the dinners I've shared with you and Jacey last night and tonight have been more fun than I've had in years. The two of you make me realize how lonely I've been. Thank you for spending some time with me."

Enthralled with his words, Rachel didn't realize his intent until it was too late. He brushed his lips against hers in a kiss as innocent as a young teenager's first experiment in romance. If she'd been prepared, Rachel was sure she would have protested. But she wasn't. So her lips clung to his, moved against them and then opened to his touch. He didn't refuse her invitation.

It was John who ended the kiss. That teasing grin of his reappeared and he murmured, "I can't wait for Friday night."

She slammed the door shut behind him and then sank against it, wanting to protest his inference. That there would be more kisses on Friday. But it was too late. He'd left.

She would have protested, she assured herself, even as she relived the feel of his lips, her fingers touching her own still-tingling ones.

Of course, she would have.

Of course.

BUD CASSIDY ROSE TO HIS feet and extended his hand.

As John grasped it, the man said, "You know, John, I'm used to David's genius in choosing the right people, but he certainly demonstrated it again when he selected you."

"That's very kind of you, Bud, but I'm not sure it's justified. Besides, as I told you Tuesday, nothing's settled, yet."

"It will be, as soon as David sees the suggestions and projections you've made. You'll have those on paper for me by Monday?"

John assured him he would, although, in truth, he planned to have them with him Friday night. In case he got a chance to show them to David.

He escorted Bud from his office, then checked his watch. Just a little after four. Last night he'd worked at the office until almost midnight. When he'd arrived home, he'd looked longingly at the house next to his, but it had been dark, both its occupants, he assumed, fast asleep.

Gathering up the papers pertaining to Wester Enterprises, he stuffed them into his briefcase, grabbed his suit coat and strode past his secretary.

"I'll see you in the morning, Beth. Go on home and spend a little extra time with your family."

He barely heard her surprised thanks as he ran for the elevator. All he could think about was getting home to see Rachel and Jacey. Telling them about his day. Hearing about theirs.

"This is crazy," he told himself as he slid behind the wheel of his Porsche. Rachel probably wouldn't even speak to him. Tuesday night, she'd warned him away.

Leaving her alone last night wouldn't be enough to convince her to change her mind. He pressed down on the accelerator. It was as if he was addicted. *Addicted to love,* he sang to himself.

The wail of a siren and flashing red lights in his rearview mirror drew him away from his startling thoughts. He immediately pulled to the side of the road.

"Good afternoon, sir. May I see your license and registration, please?" The cop standing beside his car was faultlessly polite.

"Here you are, officer."

"Could you tell me why you were going fifty miles per hour in a thirty-mile zone? Do you have an emergency?"

John couldn't read the policeman's expression because he wore mirrored sunglasses, but he didn't bother to come up with a lie. "No," he grinned ruefully. "I didn't even realize how fast I was going. I was in a hurry to get home and see—and see my family."

The officer looked from John to his license and back again. Finally, he handed the license back to John.

"I'm just giving you a warning this time, Mr. Crewes. You've got to keep it within the speed limit, or you might not make it home. Okay?"

"Thank you, officer. I'll remember."

He felt a little guilty about using Jacey and Rachel to manipulate the cop. Nor was he sure why the policeman had decided to be generous. Not that he was complaining, but he *had* been speeding.

In more ways than one.

He'd been speeding down an emotional highway with no thought to the consequences. What was he doing? Rushing home to a nonexistent family? Rachel wasn't going to welcome him with open arms. Jacey might, but not Rachel.

And did he want her to? Of course, he was attracted to her. She was a beautiful, intelligent woman. But he knew better than to expect love, commitment, "forever," from a woman.

Deliberately, he turned off into the shopping center where a deli was located. He was just having an early night. It had nothing to do with the two females next door. He purchased enough food for one, then drove home.

As a test of his will, he allowed his gaze to rove over the house next door, then turned away, feeling he was moving in slow motion. With dinner in one hand and his briefcase in the other, he slammed the car door shut with his hip and started up the short sidewalk to his door.

That's when he realized Jacey was sitting on his front porch.

So much for detachment and disinterest.

"Jacey? What are you doing over here?"

Her blue eyes were big, rounded with questions. "You didn't come home last night," she said quietly, in a hushed voice, her little chin supported by two fists as she leaned on her scrunched legs.

"Of course I did, sweetheart. I just worked late and then left this morning before you were awake. You didn't worry about me, did you?"

She nodded her head solemnly.

"I'll bet your mommy told you I was working late," John teased as he put the food and briefcase down on the porch and joined Jacey on the step.

She nodded again.

"Then what's the problem?"

"Earl said that's when he knew his daddy was gone. He didn't come home at night anymore."

He remembered from their first encounter that Earl was the one who didn't count, 'cause he didn't care about his daddy leaving. He wished Earl had kept his knowledge to himself.

"Sweetheart," he assured her as he lifted her into his lap, "I work late a lot, but I always come home."

"Always?"

"Always."

"Jacey?" Rachel's voice surprised them both and they looked across the driveway to Jacey's front porch where Rachel stood, looking up and down the street.

"Uh-oh," Jacey muttered under her breath.

"What's wrong?"

"I wasn't supposed to bother you."

"Jacey?" Rachel called again.

"We'd better answer or she'll get mad," Jacey said and then called out to her mother. "Here I am!"

John could see first the relief and then the withdrawal in Rachel. She released the door behind her and slowly came down her steps and across to his sidewalk.

"Jacey, you need to come inside." Rachel stood there, looking at her child, not him, her hand extended.

In denim shorts and a blue T-shirt, her long dark hair pulled back from her face, Rachel looked as beautiful as he'd ever seen her.

Jacey started to move, but he tightened his hold on her. "Aren't you even going to speak to me, Rachel?"

"Good evening, John. Jacey?"

John kept hold of Jacey, thus keeping Rachel only a few feet from him. "Have another bad day at school?"

"No. Jacey, come home."

He loved the sound of her voice. It was low, musical, full, as if her heart was in every word. "I don't think I'll turn her loose. I'll hold her hostage until the two of you agree to dine with me." He was teasing, of course, but Rachel glared at him.

"Release her at once, John, or I'll call the police."

"Hey, I was only teasing." He hugged Jacey and then released her. "But I can't afford another encounter with the police today."

Rachel had grabbed Jacey's hand and turned around to rush away from him, but she hesitated and said, "Another?"

"I didn't rob a bank or murder anyone, Rachel," he assured her dryly. He got the impression she was hoping he'd be thrown in jail and she wouldn't have to see him again. "I just drove a little too fast."

"Did you get a ticket?" Jacey asked, all concern.

"No, sweetheart. The officer just warned me to be more careful."

Rachel gave an elegant little snort that expressed her opinion of the officer's generosity.

"Sorry to disappoint you, Rachel."

She shot him a disdainful look, as if she had no idea what he meant. Then she tugged on Jacey's hand. "Come on, sweetie. We need to go home."

"I'd be glad to buy dinner, if you and Jacey would join me," he said, determined to give it the old college try. He stood and moved over to block her view of the deli containers on the porch behind them.

"I think you've fed us enough, Mr. Crewes. Thank you, anyway."

"John could come to our house and eat with us, Mommy. I haven't told him about Mr. Sam."

"Sorry, sweetie, but there's only enough for the two of us."

"Who's Mr. Sam?" John asked as Rachel managed to move Jacey a couple of feet along the sidewalk. He came down the steps to follow them.

Jacey's face lit up at his interest. "He's our turtle at school. Today, he got lost!"

"Got lost, did he? Must be an adventuresome creature."

Jacey screwed up her little face and said, "What's adven—what you said?"

John squatted down to her level. "I meant he must like to explore."

"That's what Mrs. Wilson said, but Earl said he ran away and wouldn't come back—like his daddy."

Ah. Now he knew why Earl had decided to share his knowledge of family dynamics. With one finger he tilted up Jacey's chin. "But Earl was wrong, wasn't he? You found Mr. Sam, didn't you?"

"Yes, he was under Mrs. Wilson's desk," Jacey told him with a giggle that brought a smile to his lips. Jacey's giggles reminded him of the fizz in soda. Irresistible. Life without hearing that giggle would be decidedly flat.

"Now you've told him about Mr. Sam, we have to go home, Jacey," Rachel said, reminding the other two of her stiff presence.

He really hadn't forgotten about her, of course—not with those long, tanned legs on view—but Jacey had claimed his attention for the moment.

"We're still on for tomorrow night?" he asked, holding his breath. The way she was acting today, he wasn't sure she'd even be speaking to him tomorrow, much less accompanying him to the Westers.

"We're going to Lisbeth's house tomorrow!" Jacey said, as if his words had reminded her of a treat.

"Yes," Rachel replied, ignoring Jacey's exclamation. Without another word, she pulled her daughter along behind her, leaving him standing on the sidewalk, watching them. At the last minute, Jacey turned to wave to him before Rachel swept her into the house.

DAMN! JOHN CRUNCHED the pages of the *Wall Street Journal* between his fingers the next morning. Who'd notified the paper that he was taking over some of Wester's accounts? It had to be Bud Cassidy. *He* certainly hadn't.

Now, if David decided he didn't want to do business with John anymore, it would look as if he'd found something disreputable or weak about John's company. No amount of reassurances or protestations to the business community would change that. David Wester's influence was too great. His withdrawal could cost John big time.

He chewed on his bottom lip, fighting the sinking feeling that filled him. He'd made a good recovery since his disastrous divorce, but he didn't know if he could survive another blow to his integrity, his reputation.

With the notice in the most important business paper in the country, there was no way he could keep David's withdrawal a secret.

Now it wasn't a question of making a lot of money. It was a question of losing everything he had.

Chapter Seven

All day long, John contemplated his dilemma.

When the *Wall Street Journal* called for an interview, he'd stalled them. He hadn't yet decided what to do. It was a tough decision.

His company had been his life for the past five years. It was the major accomplishment of his lifetime. It was also the sole support of thirty-one employees, several of whom would have difficulty finding another job.

Finally, he decided he had to talk to Rachel, make her understand what his confession to David Wester was going to do. Surely she would see how the announcement had changed everything.

After driving home, he dressed for the evening in jeans, a knit shirt and a casual sport coat. Then, with his heart beating double time, he crossed over to Rachel's house.

He rang the doorbell and waited with impatience for her to answer it. When he finally heard footsteps, he stood at attention, preparing for the battle he knew he faced.

"You're early," Rachel said first of all, and she wasn't offering praise. She was dressed in a denim skirt and a raspberry knit shirt, its scoop neck inset with some kind of lace-like thing. John didn't know what it was called, but it drew his attention to a very distracting part of her anatomy.

He cleared his throat. "Uh, I know I'm early, but I need to talk to you."

"Hi, John!" Jacey exclaimed, racing to the door to poke her head around her mother's leg.

"Hi, sweetheart. Are you ready?"

"Yes. Mommy let me wear my new shirt." Jacey pushed past her mother to stick her little chest out with pride. "See? These are from the cartoons," she explained, tracing the picture on the front of her shirt.

"You look beautiful. But I need to talk to your mommy before we go. Could you go upstairs and play for just a little while?"

"Wait, Jacey," Rachel ordered as the child nodded and turned to follow his directions. Then she looked at John. "Jacey can stay down here with you while I finish getting ready. Then we'll switch places."

"Okay."

He spent the next few minutes entertaining and being entertained by Jacey. She told him all about her day at school and he even found himself chuckling a few times. But in the back of his mind, all he could think about was the loss of his life's work.

It wasn't the money. He had enough invested to survive, and he could probably get a job with another company. But this company was all he had to show for his life. He couldn't let it be dismissed as if it didn't matter.

Rachel came down the stairs and his breathing grew more shallow. The moment of decision was at hand.

She sent Jacey up the stairs, then sat down in the chair across from him.

"What is it?"

He sought for the right words, persuasive words, that would convince Rachel to let his company survive. He couldn't find any. Finally, he blurted out, "We can't tell David the truth."

Rachel's seemingly relaxed demeanor disappeared at once. She stiffened. "What did you say?"

"Rachel, someone leaked David's decision to the *Wall Street Journal.* It wasn't me. I told Bud Cassidy we could have preliminary talks but that nothing was decided."

"So they'll just print a retraction." There was no warmth in her beautiful voice. She spoke as if there was no alternative.

"Rachel, it wasn't printed as a rumor. It was an announcement. If David withdraws two days later, it's going to look like there's something wrong with my company."

"That's ridiculous. People change their minds all the time."

"Not when the topic is millions of dollars. Not unless there's a good reason." Rachel stared at him but didn't say anything. "Rachel, if he changes his mind that fast, people will assume all sorts of horrible things. It will destroy my company."

"Don't be silly. You may lose his business, but there will be lots of other people who—"

"Would you trust your money, your life savings, your company's future, to a man a famous psychologist dumps overnight with no logical explanation?" He paused but Rachel said nothing. "Even the smallest investor will look for advice from someone else."

"Mr. Wester's influence can't be that big," Rachel insisted.

"Financially, he's got more influence than he knows what to do with. And his popularity and fame have spread in the last few years. The videos he's marketing have brought him a lot of attention."

Rachel stood to pace across the room, her arms folded about her lithe body. "This is incredible, John. You can't ask me to continue with a lie just because—"

"Because my company's existence hangs in the balance? My employees' jobs could disappear overnight? My entire career would amount to nothing?" he finished, his voice heavy with concern.

"But you don't know that he'll fire you. You're just assuming the worst."

"With good reason. Last year, one of his associates had an affair. David kicked him out on his ear."

"But we're not— I mean, we're not doing anything immoral!"

"No, not at all. Lying is always good. Highly recommended."

"You don't have to be sarcastic!" Rachel snapped.

John covered his eyes with his hands to regroup. It helped not to be able to see her. Taking down his hands, he said, "Sorry, Rachel. But you're being naive. David Wester's reputation is the foundation of his success. Just as mine is. If there is any hint of a scandal, David could lose all he's built up. He's shown himself to be ruthless in protecting what is his."

"Well, I may not have millions of dollars, or financial success weighing in the balance, John Crewes, but Jacey is more important than either of those things. I have to protect her."

"And I wouldn't ask you to do anything less, but how is it going to hurt Jacey if David believes we're married?"

"It's going to teach her to lie. I can't do it! I'm sorry, John. I realize how important this is, but I can't lie about our relationship anymore!" She stood and walked to the bottom of the stairs. "Are we still going?"

"Yes," John said, standing, his heart heavy. "I've got to make the attempt to salvage the situation if I can."

"Jacey, come on," Rachel called up the stairs. "We're leaving."

RACHEL SAT BESIDE JOHN in his Porsche without saying a word. Over and over in her head, she replayed his remarks. Surely David Wester wouldn't get rid of John without giving him a chance to show what he could do.

She had to believe that. She didn't want to be responsible for the destruction of his company. John stared straight ahead, with a stillness about his features that told her he was suffering.

After several attempts to talk to the adults, Jacey seemed to understand that something was wrong. Rachel looked over her shoulder once or twice to smile encouragingly at her daughter, but Jacey's face was growing as solemn as John's.

When they pulled into the driveway of the Westers' large home, John got out of the car and then pulled his seat forward for Jacey to follow him.

"John?" Jacey asked as she got out of the car.

"What, Jacey?"

"Are you mad?"

Rachel, walking around the hood of the car to join them, didn't know what John would answer. He had reason to be angry, since he'd gotten trapped in this situation because he wanted to help Jacey. But if he upset her child, she would hate him.

Instead, he scooped Jacey up into his arms. "Mad? No, of course not. I just had something on my mind."

"Is it all gone?" she asked anxiously, putting her arms around his neck.

"No, sweetheart. Why?"

"'Cause I want you to have a good time. If you don't, you might not go with us again."

Jacey certainly reduced everything down to its basic level. Rachel was pretty sure John wouldn't be going anywhere with them again.

Hugging her against him, John said in a low voice Rachel had to strain to hear, "Nothing would make me not want to go someplace with you, Jacey Cason. We're friends, aren't we?"

She nodded, her ponytail bouncing up and down. "But Earl said—"

John groaned and grinned at the same time—an entrancing combination, Rachel decided.

"I don't think I want to hear Earl's explanation for what a daddy does, Jacey." With his free hand, he gently pulled Jacey's head down so that he could kiss her forehead. "You just remember that you're a special girl and I'll always want to go with you."

Jacey's one-hundred-megawatt grin flowed from John to her mother. "And tonight, I can call you Daddy if I want, can't I?"

"You bet, sweetheart. Call me anything you want."

Rachel stared at John's back. If what he'd said was true, the man was facing the destruction of the most important thing in his life, and he took the time to reassure her daughter. She was still staring when he turned around.

"Ready, Rachel?" He extended his hand to take hers, and she thought about the picture they must present. A man, a woman, and their child.

When they reached the front door, John nodded for Rachel to push the doorbell. He kept her other hand clasped warmly in his. She couldn't help thinking that if it had been her teaching career that was about to be destroyed, through no fault of her own, she might not be able to face it as courageously as John Crewes.

Carol Wester opened the door. Rachel had met her a few times, but she didn't know her well.

"Oh, welcome! You're early. Well, not really, it's just that few people ever arrive on time. Come on in." She held the door wide and smiled at them. "I'm glad you could come. And Rachel, I was surprised to hear you were married. These things happen so suddenly, don't they?"

Rachel could feel John's gaze on her, but she only murmured, "Yes, they certainly do."

"Where's David?" John asked.

"Oh, he called an hour ago. He was making a connection in Chicago and they were having terrible thunderstorms. He thinks he'll be here in about—" she paused to look at her watch "—about an hour and a half, I think."

Rachel and John looked at each other, but Rachel didn't know what to say. She'd promised John could be the one to tell David. That seemed the least she could do, in the circumstances, so she agreed that air travel was hectic and followed her hostess down the hall.

As Carol led them into a sprawling, beautiful den, she said, "We won't wait on him to eat, though. I don't believe in starving, even for David. And everyone else agrees."

Everyone else?

For the first time, Rachel realized they were not the only guests. Three other couples were seated on the leather couches and chairs in front of a huge fireplace, which was filled with a basket of flowers since it was almost summer.

"Let me introduce John and Rachel Crewes and their daughter, Jacey, Lisbeth's best friend. John also just became David's financial adviser. He's probably very good at what he does, but David was impressed with his magic tricks," she added with a laugh. "Maybe we can get him to perform for us later on."

She then named the couples. Rachel's mouth went dry as she recognized the president of the local school board. *Oh, dear.* John's arm went around her waist, drawing her attention. The last pair—an older man, baldheaded with glasses, and his gray-haired wife—rose and the man extended his hand to John.

"No need for an introduction here, Carol. John and I had several meetings this week. And I can tell you I was impressed."

He then turned to Rachel. "I'm Bud Cassidy, financial officer for Wester Enterprises, and this is my wife, Ethel. We'll see a lot of each other. David's real big on social events with his employees. We're just like a big family."

"We're expanding the family this evening with a few neighbors, too," Carol explained as the doorbell rang. "You two sit down and get comfortable. Jacey, Lisbeth is waiting for you upstairs." She swept out of the room before any of them could respond.

"You want to go upstairs, Jacey?" John asked quietly.

She nodded and wriggled in his arms. He set her down and watched as she checked with her mother before leaving the room.

"Such a charming child," Ethel Cassidy said, drawing Rachel's attention.

"Thank you."

"Come sit over here by me and tell me all about you and John. Bud's been raving about that man of yours for the past two days."

Rachel cast a panicked look at John and he stepped to her side, putting an arm around her.

"She can come if I can, too. I love to hear compliments about myself," he said to Ethel with a grin. Everyone laughed, but John stuck at Rachel's side.

Not that she was about to complain. She'd need some help if Ethel's questions grew too detailed. Like how old her husband was. How long he'd lived in Kansas City. Or anything other than his eye color and what kind of car he drove... and how his lips felt, pressed to hers.

The next two hours were tense ones for Rachel. She and John stayed together as much as they could. One lady guessed they must be newlyweds, and Carol hastened to assure her she was correct. Rachel could feel the heat in her cheeks as everyone beamed at the two of them.

The school-board president's wife pressed for details about their marriage. Rachel wondered if perhaps her career was in as much jeopardy as John's, now.

John, with his arm around her, leaned over to whisper in her ear. "I'm sorry. Do you want me to tell them now?"

She shook her head no and asked Carol if she'd taken Lisbeth to see the Disney movie that had just come out. That distraction worked until the sound of footsteps coming down the hallway signaled that their host had arrived.

Feeling John tense beside her, Rachel studied him under the cover of all the greetings David Wester received. The group had swollen to nine couples plus the host and hostess, so it took several minutes for David to reach them.

Those minutes seemed to last forever as Rachel thought about what was to happen. She'd just spent two hours pretending to be John's wife. She didn't like pretense, but she liked hurting other people less. She liked waste even less. And she liked rewarding a good man with a kick in the gut a lot less.

John was a good man. He'd done his best for Jacey. She couldn't repay him with an action that would destroy him. It was hard to think amid all the talk and tension, but she just couldn't tear down all he'd built up.

"John, glad you could make it. And you must be Rachel," David Wester said, smiling at her. Much to her surprise, she recognized the face of the man before her. She'd seen ads on television for his counseling tapes. He seemed a pleasant man with gray eyes that looked deep inside you, but he was older than she'd expected Carol's new husband to be.

She managed a wobbly smile.

"Where are the girls? Upstairs?"

"Yes, they're playing."

"I'll bet you've been up to check on them several times, though, haven't you?" He grinned as she nodded. "Just like Carol. We've got a couple of terrific mothers for our girls, don't we, John?"

"Yeah, we do. Uh, David, I know you just got in, but—"

She couldn't let him do it.

Taking his arm and leaning into his shoulder, she chided him in what she hoped were wifely tones, "Now, John, you should let David eat before you tell him how much you liked working with Bud. Even if he did make you promise to rave about him as soon as you saw David."

Since Bud was standing beside David, Rachel sent him a teasing grin that had him roaring with laughter. David joined in, and Rachel hoped neither of them noticed John's stunned expression.

Feeling he was moving in slow motion, John turned to stare at Rachel. What had she just done? She'd been adamant earlier that he must tell David the truth at once. Now she was stopping him, pretending they were husband and wife.

"You can tell those two haven't been married very long," Bud said as his laughter eased. "John, the proper answer is *Yes, dear.*"

"Yes, dear," John mumbled, offering a weak grin.

"That's a phrase all us old married men have memorized," Bud assured him. "It keeps us from sleeping on the couch a lot."

There was general laughter and several comments about John preferring sharing a bed with a beauty like Rachel. He couldn't even think, much less contribute to the conversation.

"I don't need dinner, since I ate on the plane, but I would like a cup of coffee and a chance to catch my breath. And, of course, I apologize for my tardiness," David said to the room in general.

"Of course. Actually, John's so excited about the work he's begun with Bud, he wanted to talk business tonight, but I told him it would be better to wait until Monday," Rachel murmured.

She was still leaning against him, holding on to his arm, as she spoke, and he scarcely took in her words.

"Good thinking, Rachel," David replied. "I know he loves his work, but I believe a man should keep work relegated to the office. I'm sure you'll help him do that."

"I certainly will. Though Jacey is even better at that than I. Before John could even get inside the house the other day, she was in his arms telling him about Mr. Sam. Did Lisbeth tell you about the pet turtle at school?"

David shook his head no.

Rachel's hand slid down to take John's and she pulled him back down on the couch beside her. "The pet turtle in their class escaped yesterday. Jacey just knew John would be as enthralled with Mr. Sam's escapade as she." She shot him a glance filled with teasing laughter before she added, "And he was."

"You know, that's exactly the reason I chose John. He is such a good father." David went on to describe John's kindergarten visit in exhausting detail.

"What are you doing?" John muttered to Rachel under his breath. His heart was thudding and his brain was fuzzy.

"I couldn't let you do it." She didn't have time to say anything else because David asked her a question.

The rest of the evening was a nightmare. All John could think about were the repercussions of their evening. Only his brain wasn't functioning clearly enough to work things out. As much as he didn't want to tell David the truth, he didn't think it was possible to continue the lie.

Rachel, however, seemed to have done an about-face. She clung to his hand all night, leaning against him, teasing him, smiling at him. He began to think he was dreaming the entire evening. But his body's response to her touch told him it wasn't a dream.

When he was almost at the point of exploding with all the questions inside him, Rachel told him they really needed to leave to get Jacey into bed.

"What is her usual bedtime?" David asked, looking straight at John.

"Uh, nine," he guessed, panic racing through him.

"Eight o'clock, actually," Rachel corrected. "Both she and John have been lobbying for nine, trying to convince me eight's too early."

"That's Lisbeth's bedtime, too," David said. "A good time. Leaves the two of you a little time for yourselves. That's important, isn't it?"

John could only nod his head. Oh, yeah, he really enjoyed those hours after Jacey was in bed. Especially since he spent them all alone at his house. And the hours before she went to bed, too.

"Now that I've met you, Rachel, I can go ahead with some plans I've made. I think you'll be as excited about them as I am," David said, smiling at her.

Rachel's eyebrows rose. "What are they?"

"Oh, I'm not going to say now. I think I'll be ready to show you in about a week. Do you two have plans for next weekend?"

"Uh, I don't think so, do we, dear?" John asked, staring at Rachel.

"Why, no, though, of course, it's getting close to the end of the school year. I don't plan too many things in May."

"Well, this will be special. Hold next weekend open for me, okay?" Then David told them goodbye and moved across the room to talk to some of the other guests.

"What did he mean, Bud?" John asked.

"Who knows? He's a genius, but he's a little demanding at times. The money's incredible, though. Ethel and I are going to have a great retirement." The older man grinned and winked at Rachel.

She smiled and then reminded John that they had to leave. She got no objection from him. He couldn't wait to get her alone and find out why she'd changed her mind. And if she realized what she'd done.

After bidding their hostess good-night, the two of them went upstairs and collected a sleepy-eyed Jacey. It was almost ten o'clock, and she wasn't used to such late hours.

John picked her up and her head flopped down against his shoulder. "I had fun," she whispered. "Did you?"

"Oh, yeah, baby, we had a barrel of laughs," he assured her, avoiding Rachel's gaze as he offered the baby-sitter, a teenager, some money for taking care of Jacey.

With Jacey still awake, although she was fading fast, the drive home was in silence. When they pulled into John's driveway, he lifted Jacey from the back seat and followed Rachel to her front door.

"I can take her now," she told John, reaching out her arms for her child.

"There's no need. I'll carry her up."

Did she think he was going to go tamely home, ignoring what had happened this evening?

She must have read the determination in his eyes, because she shrugged her shoulders and turned and unlocked the door. After putting Jacey down on her bed, John left the child to her mother's care and went down to the living room.

He didn't have long to think. Although he already knew what had to be said. Rachel came down the stairs and stopped at the door of the room, her eyes wide.

"Come on in, Rachel. We've got some talking to do."

"I'm really tired, John. Couldn't we—"

"Nope. I have to thank you for what you did tonight. But I wish— Never mind. I hope you realize what this means."

"Of course. It means your company is safe."

"True. And I really am grateful." He cleared his throat. "It also means we'll have to move in together."

Chapter Eight

Rachel stared at him. "You're out of your head."

"No, I'm not, Rachel. We both lied to David tonight. Now there's no chance he'll keep me if I tell him the truth. So, we're going to pretend to be married."

He kept his hands in his pockets, attempting a casual stance.

Rachel turned away. "I can't do that, John. I promised myself I'd never do such a stupid thing again."

Realization struck him like a bolt of lightning. "That's how you ended up pregnant with Jacey, isn't it?"

An abrupt nod was her only answer.

"So what are we going to do?"

She released a huge sigh before turning to face him. "I don't know, unless you're willing to really marry me." She gave a cynical laugh, as if she knew her remark was ridiculous.

But for John, much to his surprise, her words were an eye-opener. He'd thought he'd never marry again, would die before he reentered the state of matrimony, but the idea of marrying Rachel and Jacey had its appeal.

"Okay," he simply agreed.

She stared at him, disbelief on her expressive face. "What did you say?"

"I agreed with you. I think we should just go ahead and marry. For Jacey's sake if nothing else."

"Marry?" she repeated, as if she still couldn't believe what she'd heard.

"Just as a . . . a pretense," he hurriedly said, fearing he saw rejection on her face. He wondered if he'd made a mistake when anger clouded her eyes.

"And just how long do you think this pretense should continue? The rest of our lives?" Rachel crossed her arms in defiance. "Don't you think that's a little too much sacrifice, even for the sake of your company?"

One hand came out of his pocket to run through his hair. She realized he always did that when he was upset. "Hell, Rachel, I don't know. Six months, a year? How long would you consider?"

"You're serious?" she gasped, taking a step closer, "You're actually serious about our getting married? John, you can't be!"

"Why can't I? You decided tonight that my company was worth saving. And I appreciate it. But now we've got to find a way out of this mess. Marriage is the only answer."

"But—but we don't— That is, there's no—"

"Romance? Love? Feelings? Did you have those things with Jacey's father?"

She nodded, although she was reluctant to answer.

"I thought I did, too, with my wife. Instead, all she had feelings for was my bank account." He stood and paced several times about the room, talking as he moved.

"Look, Rachel, let's handle this like a business arrangement. We'll marry for a minimum of one year. I'll—I'll pay you a salary and—"

"No! I won't take money for..." She didn't know what to call his suggestion. But it wasn't something you did for pay.

He moved toward her and she took several steps back.

"Why not? You'll be putting a lot of money in my pocket with Wester's account."

"It doesn't matter. I can't do that."

"Okay." He turned away and began pacing again. "Okay," he repeated. "I'll support you for a year. It will save you living expenses. Your salary can go into savings. For a year, you'll appear in public as my wife. We'll live in the same house. To the world we'll appear married."

"And to ourselves?"

"What do you mean?"

He walked toward her again, and she fought to hold her ground. The attraction they'd both felt was a danger, but she didn't want to appear a coward.

"John, I'm a mature woman, not a teenybopper. We both know we're attracted to each other. But— much as I hate to confess it—I'm a romantic. I don't think sex should be an aerobic activity. It should be about feelings."

"I'm not interested in feelings," John replied crisply, stiffening.

"I know," she said, struggling to keep her voice even while her heart sank. "And that's why I don't think your plan would work."

"It could work for a year, Rachel. I'd let you decide where our relationship should go."

"But, John, you couldn't even have a relationship with anyone else or David would fire you. You'd be stuck with a monastic existence for a year." She looked him up and down. "Somehow I don't think that kind of life would be normal for you."

That sideways grin that was so alluring appeared. "Not by choice, but I'm not a swinging bachelor, Rachel. The only difficulty would be living with such temptation."

She blushed and looked away.

"You are, you know," he continued. "And you're right about the attraction between us. We've both felt it. And with an honest-to-goodness marriage license, I don't see why either of us should suffer. But that's your decision."

Sinking her teeth into her bottom lip, she shook her head. "It's too much, John. I need time to think— without you around."

"Okay. When? Tomorrow?"

"I don't know. I can't tell you when. Just give me a few days." A few days? She'd prefer weeks, years. There was too much to consider to make such a decision overnight.

He shrugged his shoulders. "Okay. I don't have much choice, do I? My company's life hangs in the balance. Don't forget that, Rachel."

"No, I won't forget."

"Can I offer any persuasion?" he asked, a twinkle in his eyes that told Rachel just what kind of persuasion he had in mind.

"No. Definitely not," she automatically replied, but there was a yearning inside her to feel his arms around her again. That traitorous yearning was what made a decision so difficult.

She escorted him from her house and closed the door behind him. Thank goodness he hadn't argued with her. If she gave in to what her body wanted, her life would become much more complicated. And when it all ended in a year, she'd be devastated.

RACHEL SPENT THE WEEKEND hiding. Every time she wanted to go somewhere with Jacey, she would peek out the window first to see if John's car was in the driveway.

"What are you doing, Mommy?" Jacey demanded.

"Just—just checking the weather to see if you need a raincoat," she improvised.

"The sun is shining."

"Oh, so it is." Not only was the sun shining, John was in evidence, doing some kind of work on his car, without a shirt. Her gaze concentrated on the muscles of his back as he bent over the motor, making it difficult to remember what she was saying. "So—so, I don't think we should go to the store right now. It's too hot."

Jacey stared at her in puzzlement, and Rachel couldn't blame her child. She wasn't making much sense. Her mind was too full of the questions John's suggestion had raised.

"Look! There's John. I'm going to go say hello," Jacey said and was out the door before Rachel could come up with a reason to keep her inside.

Through the window, she watched John hug Jacey and start showing her something under the hood. At least John wasn't lying about his feelings for Jacey. She'd never seen a man so patient. Especially one who had no children.

That was another unanswered question. Why didn't John have children? Did he not want them? Had his wife refused to have children? She wanted to know all about his failed marriage, but she didn't have the right to ask those questions.

If she refused his request that they marry, he wouldn't ever speak to her again, much less answer questions. But if she did accept? She rushed up the stairs and began cleaning out the hall closet, the most loathsome task she could think of. Anything to keep her mind off the relentless question she couldn't forget.

Monday afternoon, after picking up Jacey, Rachel pulled into the driveway, automatically noting that John's car wasn't in his. Thank goodness teaching allowed her to arrive home before him. By the time he pulled up, she would be well protected behind her four walls.

With the curtains pulled, she worked on dinner, having sent Jacey up to her room to play. Even so, she caught herself listening for his car. When she did hear it, she couldn't resist peeking out the window at him.

He looked directly at her, as if he could see her, after he got out of his car. She drew back with a gasp. Even if she decided to marry him, it would be a marriage of convenience only. She couldn't afford to let him think she had any personal interest in him. And of course, she didn't. Definitely not.

The phone rang and she answered it, still thinking about John.

"Rachel, this is David Wester. I'm sorry to bother you at home, but has John arrived yet? I just missed him at the office."

"Uh, missed him? Oh. Oh, yes, I just heard the car in the driveway. Just a minute and I'll go get him."

"There's no rush. We can just chat until he comes in," David said pleasantly. "I'm glad I reached the right number. I got it from the school directory. John's moved in with you?"

"Um, we're kind of living in both houses right now. We only just married, you know. It's h-hard to combine two households."

"Yes, I guess it is."

She had to get free of the phone. If she didn't run over to John's house and drag him back to hers, he'd never answer the phone.

"Sorry, David, I've got something in the oven and it's burning." Without waiting for him to answer, she laid down the phone and raced for the front door.

Thirty seconds later, she was pounding on John's front door. He swung it open as he loosened his tie and unbuttoned the top button of his shirt with one finger.

"Rachel. What a surprise."

He didn't act surprised, or particularly happy about her appearance. She didn't have time to think about that now.

"John, hurry. David is on the phone."

"My phone didn't ring," John assured her, a frown on his face.

"No! *My* phone. He thinks we live together, remember?"

"Damn!" John exclaimed and took off at a run.

"He thinks you've just pulled into the driveway," she shouted after him. Then she walked slowly after him. There was no need for her to hurry now.

By the time she reached her kitchen, John had hung up the phone, but his hand remained on the receiver and he was staring into space.

"Is everything all right?"

"Yeah, great. At least I didn't have a heart attack."

"What are you talking about?"

"My mad dash between our houses. Rachel, I've tried to give you time, but you've got to make up your mind. Either I go to him and tell him the truth and destroy my company, or the two of us get married."

"You said you'd give me time," she protested.

He shoved his fingers through his hair. "I did give you time. I gave you the entire weekend. Now it's time to fish or cut bait."

"Oh, that's romantic!" she retorted in disgust.

He froze and then grinned, his eyes lighting up. "You want romance?"

She recognized her mistake at once. "No! No, that's not what I meant. It was just—just an inelegant way to express yourself."

"I can be more elegant," he promised, as he started walking toward her.

"No. No, I don't want you to be more—more— Stop, John!"

"Hi, John!" Jacey exclaimed from the stairs just as John reached Rachel.

Rachel breathed a sigh of relief as John released her and went to hug Jacey.

"Hi, little one. How was your day?"

"It was fun. Did you know we're going to have a family picnic at the end of school? You can come, can't you? You said you'd be my daddy when I asked."

"Of course I can come, can't I, Mommy?" John asked, cocking one eyebrow at Rachel.

"Yes, but I'm not your mommy."

"I know," he replied, his gaze emphasizing that knowledge.

Desperate to change the subject, she asked, "What did David want?"

"He wants us to attend the Charity Ball, Friday night," John said, but he was tossing Jacey in the air at the same time, as if his request were perfectly natural.

"What?" Rachel moved closer to the other two. "Stop, John. Say that again."

"You're always telling me to stop," he complained.

Rachel closed her eyes to hide her irritation. Then she asked, "What charity ball?"

"The big one they hold every year. You've read about it, haven't you?"

"Well, yes, but—"

"David bought tickets for us. He likes the people associated with him to support the charities."

Rachel stared at him. He thought she could afford to go to the social event of the year? He thought she had a ball gown in her closet that would cost more than her annual food budget? And diamonds to go with it? The man was insane!

"I can't do that."

"Rachel, be reasonable. If you've made other plans, you'll just have to cancel them."

Almost hysterical, she said in exasperation, "You mean just cancel my date?"

John's happy-go-lucky smile disappeared. He set Jacey on the floor and grabbed Rachel's shoulders. "What date? Who are you dating?"

She pulled out of his grasp and crossed the room, folding her arms over her chest. "That's none of your business."

"It might be," he said gruffly as he followed her. "If you're dating someone, David might get word of it. You could ruin the whole plan."

"What plan?" Jacey demanded, yanking on the leg of John's trousers.

Momentarily distracted from Rachel, John knelt down to Jacey's level. "That's a secret, sweetheart. Can you keep a secret?"

"Yes. Real good." She nodded her head, too, to make sure he believed her.

"Well, Mommy and I have a plan where I'd be your daddy for a whole year."

Jacey frowned and cast an anxious look at her mother.

"What's wrong? Wouldn't you like that?" John questioned, and Rachel couldn't help but like the touch of uncertainty in his voice.

"Yes, but—but I don't got enough money. I gave you all the money I got."

John looked up at Rachel, but she wasn't sure what his expression meant. Then he scooped Jacey into his arms. "You don't understand, little one," he said after he hugged her. "Being your daddy is so special that *I'm* going to pay *you.*"

The radiance on Jacey's face almost brought tears to Rachel's eyes. She looked away.

"So, how much will you charge me?" John asked.

"John—" Rachel began in protest. She didn't want her child to believe that there was a monetary value on such a thing.

He held up his hand. "Let Jacey answer. I might not be able to afford her, you know."

Still beaming, Jacey, with both arms around his neck, said, "I don't want no money, John. If I can have you as my Daddy for longer, I'll be happy."

"Then we'll all be happy, sweetheart," he assured her and kissed her on the cheek. "Speaking of money, I have something for you, Jacey, if your mother doesn't mind, and this seems a good time to give it to you." He reached inside his coat pocket and brought out a small booklet.

"What's that?" Jacey asked, taking it from him, a puzzled look on her face.

"It's the money you paid me."

"No, John, this is a book," Jacey explained, frowning.

"Look inside. See that writing? It says three dollars and sixty-seven cents. The bank with its name on the cover is keeping your money, and it will make your money grow. And since you don't have to hire a daddy anymore, you can save more money."

"I give my money to you? And you put it in the bank?"

"Right. Okay?" Although he asked Jacey, he was looking at Rachel.

She nodded. His action was honorable and would teach Jacey about money at the same time. She couldn't object.

"Will you find money behind my ears so's I can put it in the bank?" Jacey asked, a speculative gleam in her eye.

"Jacey, I explained that John didn't really find that money there," Rachel protested, recognizing that Jacey was borrowing a page from John's book of manipulation.

John grinned. "You never know, Jacey." He set the little girl down. "Now, you run upstairs and play and Mommy and I will work out the details of our plan."

Rachel kept silent until she heard the door of her daughter's room close. "Thank you for the savings account, John. But please don't encourage her to accept money from you."

"An occasional quarter won't hurt, Rachel. And you have to keep her believing in magic, don't you? After all, it got her a daddy."

She was supposed to be thankful that her child's naïveté had gotten them into this mess? That thought brought her back to John's last words to Jacey. "What did you mean, telling Jacey we were going to work out the details? As if everything is settled?"

"It is. But first, let's talk about this date Friday night. Who is the guy?"

Rachel moved behind the couch. She didn't like the predatory look in John's eye. "There is no date."

He'd been stalking her, but her answer stopped him dead in his tracks. "What? You made that up?"

"Not—not on purpose. I was just responding to your ridiculous presumption."

"And what presumption was that?" he asked as he started moving toward her again.

She backed away. "That I could go to the Charity Ball Friday evening."

"But you'll have to, Rachel, if we're going to continue our little charade. And we are, aren't we? You're not going to destroy everything I've worked for over one little evening out, are you? Jacey approves," he told her, his manner confident again.

His last remark stopped her retreat. In a flash, she started toward him, fire in her eyes. "Thank you for reminding me! How dare you tell Jacey what your plans were before I agreed! How could you mislead her like that? Promising to be her daddy for a year. Do you think she has any concept of time? She doesn't know how long a year is!"

"Jacey? You've got to be kidding," John protested. He reached out and caught the finger she was shaking at him. "Come on, Rachel, Jacey understands a year."

In all honesty, she knew he was right. Jacey understood a year. What she wouldn't understand was John walking away from them when that year ended. And that was the part Rachel would have difficulty with, too. How did one put a time limit on the heart?

"That's not what's worrying you, is it?" John asked softly as he pulled her to him. Rachel leaned against his chest, her head bowed, unsure how much to reveal.

"I'm afraid she'll be hurt."

He tipped her chin up so he could see her face. "Rachel, I promise I'll try not to hurt her. And if we're honest with her, I don't think we will."

She read honesty in his eyes. And caring...for Jacey. She couldn't ask for anything else. Although her lips trembled, she nodded. "Okay."

Her sudden capitulation took him by surprise. But not her. She'd known since Friday night that she couldn't say no to him. She'd made her choice when she'd stopped him from revealing the truth. It had just taken her a while to admit it.

"Okay, what?" he demanded.

"Okay, we'll have a year's agreement."

"You mean you'll marry me." He made it a statement, not a question.

She nodded anyway.

"When?"

"I don't know. I guess as soon as possible." As if talking about the intimacy of marriage made her realize how close to each other they stood, she jerked away from his hold. "If we're going to—to do it, we should do so immediately."

"Right. I'll, um, I'll check on the requirements. Do you know anything about them?"

"No. You're the one who's been married," she reminded him.

"Oh, yeah. There was a waiting period, I believe. Uh, maybe we should consider Oklahoma."

"Oklahoma?" Rachel questioned, wondering if he'd lost his mind. What did Oklahoma have to do with anything?

"Yeah, we could get married tomorrow in Oklahoma. That's what we'll do."

"I have to teach tomorrow," she reminded him.

"Call in sick. I'll make arrangements for a private plane to fly us to the closest city, then fly us back. We could do it in two or three hours. I might only miss half a day at work, which is good, because I have a lot to do. Then, we'll—"

"Wait just a minute!"

He stopped in midsentence, seemingly surprised by her interruption. "What's wrong?"

"Just like that? I'm supposed to call in sick?"

"Well, you can't exactly tell them you're eloping since you're already supposed to be married."

"And what are you going to tell your office?"

He shrugged. "I'm the boss. I don't have to give excuses."

"What about Jacey?"

"You want her to come with us?"

"No! I can't leave her here while I go out of town, though."

"Why not? She'll be at school all day, as usual."

"What if she got sick? They wouldn't be able to find me." Somewhere, Rachel knew, there had to be a reasonable excuse not to elope tomorrow.

"She's perfectly healthy. But we'll tell her if she needs you to have them call my office, and they'll get in touch with us."

"And then they'd know I wasn't really sick," she declared triumphantly.

"Rachel, that's not going to happen. And if it does, they won't fire you for that. If they do, though, I'm supporting you, so what difference does it make?"

"That's my professional career, just as your company is your professional career, John. Are you willing to throw your career away? Seems to me we're going to great lengths because you aren't."

"You're right. I apologize. But I don't know what else to do. We can't afford to wait, Rachel."

With a sigh, she capitulated—again. "I know, I know."

He took hold of her shoulders, caressing her through her blouse. "Everything will be all right, Rachel. We'll get the marriage taken care of and then we can go Friday night with a clear conscience.''

Friday night. Reminded of what had started their marathon argument, Rachel sighed again. "I can't go Friday night.''

Chapter Nine

"Nervous?"

Rachel took a quick glance at John's face and then looked away. She didn't want to admit how much their plans, made the previous night, disturbed her. After all, she'd agreed to the marriage.

"We're almost there," he added when she said nothing in response to his question.

"Yes."

They had boarded a small plane just as soon as they'd dropped Jacey at kindergarten with a note in her pocket that gave John's office number, should she need her mother. For an emergency, of course.

The plane started its descent and Rachel thought the butterflies in her stomach had turned into bombers. She clenched her fists in her lap, then wished she hadn't when John reached over to hold them. She knew he was trying to reassure her, but she didn't need his touch. In fact, his touch was a complication she didn't even want to think about.

Once they were on the ground, she released her seat belt and stood. John guided her down the steps, after thanking the pilot and reminding him they would be returning in about an hour.

"This trip must be costing you a fortune," she muttered.

"That doesn't matter. You're doing me a big favor, and we both know it. Quit worrying about the money. And that goes for the clothes for Friday night, too. I don't intend to argue that issue again."

She sighed. They had had a rousing argument last night when she'd again said she couldn't go to the ball on Friday. John had worn her down, insisting that buying her outfit would be like giving an employee a uniform.

Well organized, John whisked them away in a rental car, a map in his hand showing the location of the justice of the peace where he'd made an appointment for their marriage.

Rachel sat beside him, feeling as if she were caught up in a bad dream.

"What happened to Jacey's father?"

John's sudden question immediately took her mind away from the marriage ceremony. "That's none of your business."

"I think it is. I'm going to be Jacey's stepfather in a few minutes. I ought to know what happened."

"You're not really going to be her stepfather. I mean, it's just a temporary thing."

"While we're married, I'm her stepfather." His tones were firm, allowing no disagreement.

"Fine. But that doesn't mean you should know all the dirty details of my past life. You haven't told me about your marriage."

"What do you want to know?"

"I don't want to know anything!" That wasn't true, but she wasn't about to let him think she had spent any time dwelling on the woman he used to love.

"Good. Now, tell me about Jacey's father. Does he send child support? And does Jacey ever see him?"

"No."

"No to what?"

"No, he doesn't send child support and no, she never sees him."

She watched him take his eyes off the road to stare at her before quickly returning his attention to his driving. "You haven't had any help from him at all?"

Looking out the window so she couldn't see his reaction, she briefly, unemotionally, outlined Jacey's past history. "When I told Dirk I was pregnant, he asked me to leave. He accused me of sleeping with someone else, said he would challenge his paternity if I tried to get anything out of him."

She expected him to ask if Dirk's accusations were true. Her parents had asked when she'd gone to them. But John surprised her.

"But that wasn't true, was it? So why didn't you take him to court and at least get some financial help?"

"How do you know it wasn't true?" she asked faintly.

He turned off the road into a driveway and parked by the sign advertising marriages before he answered. Then he turned in his seat and looked into her eyes. "Because you don't like lies, Rachel Cason. And because when you love someone, like Jacey, you do it with your entire heart."

Tears flooded her eyes and she ducked her head, hoping he wouldn't notice.

"So why didn't you take him to court?" he asked again.

"I was all alone, young, hurt. I didn't want to have anything to do with him ever again."

"Surely your parents advised you to do so? They must have realized what a financial burden raising a child on your own would be."

"My parents thought it was possible he'd told the truth, and they were concerned with the embarrassment it might cause them." She couldn't keep the bitterness out of her voice. Their betrayal had hurt more than Jacey's father's.

John muttered something under his breath and she flashed him a quick glance before looking away again.

"So you managed on your own? How old were you?"

"Almost nineteen."

"How did you do it?"

She shrugged her shoulders, as if those years had been easy. "I had some scholarships that helped pay the tuition and I took out student loans. I'll have them paid off after I teach school this summer."

"You teach in the summer, too? Doesn't Jacey need you to spend time with her?"

He'd touched a raw wound. She hated not spending the summers with Jacey. It was a time of renewal that she needed. But she also needed to relieve them of the debt her education had cost. "I don't have a choice!" she snapped. "I have to pay off the debt!"

He touched her shoulder. "You're right. That was a dumb question."

She kept her head turned from him. If he couldn't see her face, then he wouldn't know how much his words had disturbed her.

JOHN FELT LIKE A MONSTER, upsetting Rachel on her wedding day. Her first wedding day. When she'd said last night that he was the only one who'd been married, he realized she was an unmarried mother.

As he'd tossed and turned during the night, he kept trying to imagine the circumstances that would cause a man to walk away from Rachel when she was carrying his child. He couldn't picture it.

Now he had his answer.

"Come on, Rachel. Let's go get married."

Still without looking at him, she opened her car door. He reached into the back seat and picked up the box he'd ordered. Opening it, he took out a small bouquet. At least she'd have flowers for her wedding.

He rounded the car and held out the bouquet to her. Finally she looked at him, with a flash of surprise and gratitude that lit him up inside like a neon sign.

"Thank you."

"My pleasure. By the way, I don't think I've told you how beautiful you look today." Even if she hadn't, he would have said so, but Rachel made it easy. She was knock-down gorgeous in a champagne-colored silk suit. Her dark hair formed a glorious cloud of curls around her face.

With flushed cheeks, she gave him another quick glance before accepting his compliment. Then she started up the sidewalk, as if she wanted to get on with the procedure.

He followed her, but slowly. She was beautiful. And lovely inside as well as out. And he adored her child. Which didn't explain the clenching of his gut. But he knew the reason. Damn, he was unhappy about marrying again. Even to save his company.

His wife had taught him a tough lesson. He'd thought himself desperately in love when he'd waited for her at the altar in an elegant church wedding. But it had all been a lie. Six years later, she'd tried to destroy him.

How much power did this wedding give to Rachel? And would she ever use it against him? He didn't want to know the answer today. Otherwise he wouldn't be able to go through with it.

Feeling like a rank coward, he caught up with Rachel and they entered the house together.

The justice of the peace was an elderly man whose wife assisted with the ceremony, playing taped music at appropriate times and offering the use of a veil. Rachel refused, and the ceremony began.

"I now pronounce you man and wife," the man intoned after the vows were taken. "You may now kiss the bride."

Rachel looked at him, as if not sure he intended to take advantage of that custom. Hell, it was the best part. He wasn't about to pass up an opportunity to hold her.

He wrapped his arms around her and lowered his mouth to hers. She didn't resist. In fact, he wasn't sure but he thought she welcomed his caress. The magic he'd felt when he'd kissed her before seemed to have increased and he lost all awareness of the time or the place until the JP touched him on the arm.

"Ahem, excuse me, Mr. Crewes, but we have another couple ready to be married."

John felt like a teenager caught by his girlfriend's father. Rachel's cheeks were red, too, indicating she was embarrassed by their marathon kiss. John, with a quick payment, including a big tip, got them out of there promptly. The deed was done. That was the important thing.

RACHEL STUDIED THE slender gold band on her third finger. John had apologized after the ceremony, saying that was all he'd been able to manage before they left town, but he'd get her something nicer right away.

She didn't want anything else. Something plain and unpretentious suited her. Besides, diamonds for a business arrangement just didn't seem right.

"You've been quiet. Are you okay?" John asked just before they landed in Kansas City again.

"I'm fine."

"Good. We'll go have lunch now. One of my favorite restaurants is down on the Plaza. Is that okay with you?"

"I thought you needed to work."

"I changed my mind. A person doesn't get married every day."

He smiled at her, and Rachel looked away. She wished he'd be rude and curt. It would make it easier not to fall under his sway. She was determined not to let her hormones or whatever had betrayed her with Jacey's father do the same with John.

The meal was an agony. The restaurant was lovely, the food excellent, the waitress perfect. Her dinner companion was the most charming man alive. And she fought his every smile.

By the time the meal was finished, his smile had a terse edge to it. She regretted upsetting him. But she couldn't trust her heart to this man. After all, in a year, he'd be gone.

"Come on," he muttered as they left the restaurant. Since she was walking in step with him, she couldn't imagine what he meant. She had an inkling when he led her to the most exclusive store on the Plaza, Hall's.

"What are you doing?"

"We're going shopping for your dress for Friday night."

"We most certainly are not!" she snapped, trying to disengage her arm from his hold.

"Yes, we are. I can't take off the rest of the week, and I suspect it would be difficult for you, too. It only makes sense to shop now."

"I don't want—"

He pulled her to an abrupt stop and turned her to face him. "Rachel, we've already argued about this, and you agreed it was like a uniform. There's no point in doing this thing halfway. We're married. Husbands buy their wives clothes."

But they weren't really married. She knew it and he knew it. And that was why she didn't want him to buy her anything. She couldn't argue that point, however. He was right. If they were going to create this fabrication, they had to go all the way.

"Yes," she said with a sigh, her head down.

"Will it be so horrible, buying a new dress?" he teased, some of his good humor seemingly restored with her capitulation.

"No, of course not," she assured him, trying for a smile herself, but it didn't feel like a huge success.

Without another word, he led her into the department store. Within minutes, it seemed half the store employees were racing around to do his bidding. The gowns they presented to her were incredibly beautiful. But she knew her choice the moment they brought it out. A sapphire-blue silk, it had large puffed sleeves, an elongated, ribbed bodice that came to her hips and then flared into a full skirt. The neckline was cut straight across, low but not indiscreet. It was perfect.

John seemed to agree with her. "Try on that one, Rachel. I think it will look spectacular on you."

When she emerged from the dressing room, John was in deep consultation with one of the saleswomen. Rachel intended to wait patiently for his attention, although she was eager to see his reaction to the gown. However, the saleslady noticed her at once and motioned to John.

He came toward her with a gleam in his eyes that told her he approved. Taking her hands in his, he asked, "What do you think?"

"It—it's lovely."

"We'll take it," he told the saleslady over his shoulder.

"Just like that? John, did you look at the price?" she whispered urgently. She had. The gown amounted to almost two months' salary for her.

"They're bringing up some shoes for you to try on with it. And a few other things."

He added the last so casually, she didn't even think about his meaning until they began a long parade of casual and business clothes.

"John, what are you doing?" she whispered frantically, trying to avoid being overheard by the saleswomen.

"Just amplifying your wardrobe a little, Rachel. You're going to need more clothes for all the social occasions. It will be simpler to buy them now, instead of having to make extra trips every time something comes up."

His words were logical but the result was over-whelming. She felt like a doll being dressed and re-dressed over and over again.

"It's such a pleasure to work with you, Mrs. Crewes. Some of our ladies are difficult to fit, but you're a perfect size ten," the saleslady enthused.

"Thank you. But I don't think we're going to buy a lot. I shouldn't be taking up so much of your time," she said hurriedly.

"Oh, Mr. Crewes gave us specific instructions. Now, come along and show that pantsuit to him. What a wonderful husband you have."

Rachel was growing more agitated by the moment. Nothing she said seemed to have any effect on John. She felt like she was standing in the path of a large steamroller. When she came out of the dressing room, there was a shoe salesman waiting with about ten boxes of shoes. She'd already tried on the shoes to match her gown. Now what?

"Mr. Sanders thought some of these styles might go with the other outfits you've been trying on," John said with a smile—as if his behavior was perfectly normal.

Rachel looked at the beaming shoe salesman, the salesladies standing around with several hangers in each hand, at her new husband, who was assuming everything was wonderful, and she wanted to scream.

"May I speak to—to my husband privately for a moment?" she asked all the salespeople, a smile, al-beit a small one, on her face.

"Yes, of course," they assured her and hustled ten feet away to stand in a circle, pretending not to watch.

"John, what are you doing?" she whispered, her back to their audience.

"I'm buying you some pretty things."

"John, this is totally unnecessary."

"We've discussed the clothing situation before, Rachel. You don't need this kind of wardrobe to teach school. You only need it as my wife. It's the right thing for me to provide it for you."

"I understand that, but a gown for Friday night is all that is necessary at the moment. You're buying me an entire wardrobe."

"It's more practical this way," he told her, but he didn't quite meet her gaze.

"I don't think that's your only reason. Are you ashamed of the way I look?"

His surprise reassured her. His touch did even more as he reached out with both hands to caress her shoulders. "Don't be absurd, Rachel. You know I think you're beautiful. It's not that big a deal. I have lots of money and you're doing me a favor. I'm trying to repay the debt."

What could she say? He'd managed to save her pride and use logic. Even if she wasn't sure she was getting the entire story. Licking her lips, she finally said, "Okay, but let's keep it to a minimum. This is costing a lot of money."

He readily agreed and then sent her off to the dressing room to try on more clothes. Somehow, she feared she'd lost total control of the situation with her agreement.

An hour later, she came out of the dressing room in her own clothes. "John, other than the ball gown, I think the ecru pantsuit and the turquoise dress would be nice. But the rest isn't necessary." She spoke firmly, determined not to let any interest in the other magnificent clothes creep into her voice.

"We're buying those," he assured her with a smile.

"Thank you," she said, surprised by his easy capitulation.

"Now, I think we should buy Jacey something new, too. After all, she's going to have to put up with me as much as you will."

"John, really, that's not necessary."

"Yes, it is. Come on."

"But where are our packages?" She looked around, suddenly noticing that the salespeople weren't hovering around them anymore.

"Oh, they're having everything delivered."

"There wasn't that much, just the three outfits and the pair of shoes for the ball gown."

"It will be easier than having to carry it. And we'll add something for Jacey to it."

John had so much fun in the children's department, Rachel could hardly bear to put restraints on him. But she did. He bought several outfits for Jacey, and a big stuffed lion that she knew her daughter would love.

Then, while the saleslady was writing up the ticket, he wandered over to the baby clothes. "Was Jacey ever this small?" he asked, fingering a newborn's sleeper.

"Yes. It's hard to believe, isn't it?"

He continued to admire the tiny clothing until they were ready to depart.

When they were out in the warm sunshine again, Rachel decided it was her turn to ask questions.

"Why didn't you and your wife have children? You're so good with them and you obviously enjoy them."

She could tell by the expression on his face that he didn't want to answer her question. But she'd answered his. Turnabout was fair play.

Chapter Ten

They reached the car before John answered Rachel's question. After fastening his seat belt, he looked at her. "Why do you say I'm good with kids?"

"Come on, John. You're wonderful with Jacey."

"Jacey's special."

"You're not going to get her mother to disagree with you," she told him with a laugh, "but it's more than that."

He shrugged, dismissing her compliment. "I've never been around children before. My wife didn't want children, at least not right away, and I agreed. Seems to me they complicate your life."

"Oh, yes," Rachel confirmed in heartfelt tones. "But I wouldn't trade anything for Jacey."

He gave her his sexy sideways grin. "Neither would I."

They drove to Jacey's school in silence and relative harmony. Rachel was still a little uncomfortable with the spending spree they'd had, although she knew John didn't consider three outfits in that category. But she was sure Jacey would love what John had bought her.

The lion was riding in the back seat, waiting for Jacey's arrival. Rachel dismissed the small nudge of envy she felt that John could buy something like that for her daughter when she couldn't. She wasn't going to ruin Jacey's fun with such selfish thoughts.

John remained in the car while she went inside the child-care center to get Jacey. Her daughter was full of questions about her day since she knew Rachel was spending it with John. They'd kept details to a minimum, not telling Jacey they were getting married. They would explain everything tonight. At least, she hoped they'd figure out how to explain everything.

"John came to pick me up, too?" Jacey asked, thrilled to have his company.

"Yes, sweetie. And we went shopping."

"What for?"

"Well, I needed a new dress for Friday night. And then, if you'll look in the back seat, you'll see something John thought you needed."

Jacey stood on tiptoe as they approached John's Porsche. The stuffed animal practically filled the small back seat. Jacey's eyes widened in surprise.

"It's a lion!" she squealed to John as he got out of the car.

"It is," he agreed solemnly, "and I think it needs a home. Do you have room for him?"

Jacey turned her little face toward her mother. "Do we, Mommy? I can keep him in my room."

"Well, if you think he won't eat too much," Rachel agreed.

"Mommy! He's not real!" Jacey replied, grinning from ear to ear.

"Okay, then, he can come home with us."

Jacey hugged first her mother and then John, throwing her arms around his neck as he knelt to receive his reward.

Once they were on their way home, John cleared his throat. "Um, there's something we haven't discussed."

Rachel lifted her eyebrows. "I would imagine there are a lot of things we haven't discussed."

"Yes, but this one is going to arise as soon as we get home."

"You mean telling Jacey about today?" She glanced over her shoulder to see her child was engrossed in the stuffed animal.

"No. I mean, moving."

It took her a minute to realize the significance of his remark. Everything had happened so fast that she hadn't thought through all the changes that were about to occur. "Oh. I don't suppose you'd consider moving into our house?"

That sideways grin again. "Rachel, my house is paid for, updated, has a pool. You're renting, the house is in disrepair and is smaller, too."

Everything he said was true, but she was reluctant to give up the home she and Jacey had made. Somehow, standing in front of the justice of the peace had seemed far less significant than moving.

"Yes, of course. But... but is it necessary for us to make such a drastic change today?"

"When would you suggest? Next Christmas?"

She almost agreed with him before she realized he was teasing her. With a grimace, she said, "No, I guess not."

"You can just move a few things tonight, whatever you'll need for tomorrow, because we've had a long day. Then we'll use the next few evenings and the weekend to get really settled.''

His plan was sensible, but she looked over her shoulder again at her daughter. Explaining it to Jacey might not be as easy.

As if he read her mind—a disconcerting thought— he said, "Don't worry about telling Jacey. She'll like the idea.''

When they pulled into the driveway and got out of the car, Jacey was concentrating on the stuffed animal. John helped her get it out of the car.

"Say, Jacey, let's take Mr. Lion to my house. He'll have more room there.''

Rachel recognized at once the disappointment Jacey quickly hid. "Okay. He'd probably like to live with you.''

John knelt down to Jacey's level. "I don't think he'd like it so much without you. How about if you come live with me, too?''

Jacey backed up to lean against Rachel's legs. "Thank you, but my mommy and me stick together.''

"I know. I was planning on your mommy coming, too.''

"You were?" Jacey asked in surprise. After a quick glance at her mother, Jacey moved over to John. "Have you asked her?" she whispered.

John nodded.

"What did she say?''

"She said yes.''

Jacey erupted into a wild cheer.

John grinned at Rachel as he stood. Then he extended a hand to Jacey. "Let's go choose your bedroom.''

Rachel was surprised when he grabbed her hand, as he and Jacey headed for his house.

"Come on, Rachel. You get to choose a bedroom, too."

"We each get our own room?" Jacey asked, skipping excitedly at his side.

"You bet."

"John," Jacey panted, pulling on his hand.

"What, sweetheart?"

"If I'm very good, can I swim in your pool? Just once?"

Rachel bit her bottom lip as John assured Jacey she was welcome to use his pool. Her child hadn't had all that many treats in her young life. The thought occurred to Rachel that at the end of their year, Jacey might have trouble adjusting to the austere life they would return to. True as that might be, she couldn't deny her daughter the opportunity to have some fun while it was offered.

They spent the next several hours carting belongings from Rachel's house to John's. A four-bedroom house, it had a guest room downstairs and the master and two additional bedrooms upstairs. John suggested Jacey and Rachel take the other two rooms near his. He even offered Rachel the master bedroom, but she refused. She and Jacey would share the hall bath while John used the bath attached to his bedroom.

Rachel was relieved. That would eliminate any embarrassing scenes. She hurried to unpack, hoping to dismiss the images in her head of John stepping out of a shower or shaving in front of the mirror.

"Mommy!" Jacey called, interrupting her mother's thoughts.

"Yes, dear?"

"You have a ring." Jacey pointed to the gold band on Rachel's left hand.

The moment of truth was at hand. Rachel sat down on the bed in her new room and took Jacey on her lap. "Yes. Since John is going to be your daddy for a year, we had to get married, you know. That's what people do before they live together."

Jacey nodded, as if she understood completely. Then she said, "Ellen's mommy lives with her boyfriend. They didn't get married."

"How do you know?"

"'Cause we asked her if he was her new daddy. She said he was just her mommy's boyfriend."

"Yes, well, sometimes people do that, but it's not a good idea." Rachel shuddered as she thought of her own past and her daughter's future.

"Everything okay?" John asked, having appeared in the doorway.

"John, you and Mommy got married!" Jacey exclaimed. She slid off Rachel's lap and ran to hug John's knees. "You really *are* my new daddy."

"That's right, Jacey."

"For a year!" Rachel reminded them both sharply.

"But we're not going to tell anyone that, are we, Jacey?" John said, casting a frown Rachel's way.

"No. I don't want this year to ever end," Jacey said.

The sound of a big truck stopping out front distracted all of them. Rachel stepped to the window.

"My heavens, that's a huge truck for our purchases."

"Yeah, well, I'm sure they're making other deliveries after us. Why don't you start dinner, if you're sure you want to cook? Jacey and I are getting hungry."

He had offered to take them out to dinner, but Rachel had refused. She had grocery-shopped over the weekend and needed to use her supplies before they went bad.

"Okay."

She went down to the kitchen as the doorbell rang, but left John and Jacey to let the deliveryman in. As she inspected the kitchen, she noticed the deliveryman's heavy tread leaving the house. Good. It was just the three of them again. She was still nervous around strangers.

She was still nervous around John, too, but that couldn't be helped.

Then she heard the deliveryman enter the house again. That was strange. Their purchases couldn't have needed two trips unless the man was frail. Her attention drawn from the cooking, she listened as the man went out again.

She moved into the hallway, looking out the front storm door, watching the deliveryman approach his truck. Subconsciously she heard Jacey giggling upstairs. She enjoyed being with John. Rachel hoped he wouldn't tire of a five-year-old's company.

Instead of entering the cab of the truck, the man picked up a load of boxes and set them on his cart. Rachel's eyes narrowed in thought, noting that those boxes looked quite similar to the shoe boxes of the ten pairs of shoes she'd tried on.

Suddenly she whirled and took the stairs two at a time, calling as she ran, "John Crewes!"

He and Jacey appeared at the top of the stairs just as she reached them. "Yes, Rachel?"

"What have you done?"

"What are you talking about?"

"Don't play innocent with me!" She pushed past him and ran to her bedroom door. There were boxes on her bed. She pulled open the closet door and discovered her closet full of plastic-bagged hangers holding all the beautiful clothes she'd tried on.

John and Jacey stood in the doorway, both of them grinning. "Surprise," John murmured just before he had to move out of the way of the deliveryman.

Stunned, she stared at him, finding it difficult to comprehend what he'd done. The presence of the stranger snapped her out of her trance.

"Please, return all this to your truck."

The man came to a halt, surprise on his face.

"Don't pay any attention to her," John said, stepping toward her.

The man look confused. "Sir, I—"

"It's all right. I paid for everything and I want it all delivered. This is my house." He was still smiling, which irritated Rachel all the more.

"Mommy, don't you like all the pretty things?" Jacey asked.

"No! No, I don't! And I won't keep them!"

"Does that mean I can't keep mine, too?" Jacey asked, her usual exuberance missing from her voice.

Feeling like a heel, Rachel sank to her knees and hugged Jacey to her. "No, of course not, sweetie. Yours were gifts from John. You can keep them."

"So why can't you accept a few gifts, too?"

John stood beside her, looking down at her. She didn't want to answer his question. But she had to.

"Because it's too much."

Before he could answer, the deliveryman stuck out a clipboard. "That's all of it, sir. If you'll just sign by the *X*."

Rachel looked at her bed, covered in boxes. Her closet was full of more clothing than she'd ever owned in her life. In one day, her life had been turned completely upside down. She was moving, she was married, and she was overwhelmed with "things"— "things" she'd never been able to afford.

FOR THE FIRST TIME SINCE John had known Rachel, she cried. Sinking down onto the floor, she stared at her bed and tears rolled down her cheeks.

John didn't know what to do. His ex-wife had cried frequently, using tears as a weapon. Rachel, however, had withstood every adversity proudly, with her head raised.

Until he bought her a new wardrobe.

Damn. He'd wanted to make her happy, to thank her for what she'd done for him. And maybe to justify what he was doing to her and her child. He hadn't wanted to make her cry.

"Jacey, why don't you go play with your lion and let me talk to your mom, okay?"

"But she's crying. Mommy never cries," Jacey insisted, her voice shaking.

Like a retired racehorse hearing the call to the gate, Rachel lifted her head and extended a hand to her daughter. "I'm okay, baby. Really, I am. Go—go play, and I'll get dinner ready."

Minding her mother, Jacey left the room, and John took Rachel's outstretched hand and pulled her to her feet.

"Look, Rachel, I was only trying to say thank-you. You've done a tremendous thing for me, and for the people who work for me. Didn't you think I'd be grateful?"

She was recovering quickly. "Grateful? If I'd saved the nation, maybe this would be justified. All I agreed to do was live in your house for a year."

"It's more than that and you know it, Rachel. Maybe I did overdo it a little, but I can guarantee you, Carol Wester has a much larger wardrobe."

"So you're competing with David Wester?"

"No! I'm not competing. But I didn't want you to feel out of place, or at a disadvantage." After hearing her tale of her treatment at Jacey's father's hands, he also wanted to pamper her, to take care of her. Temporarily, of course. But he wasn't about to tell her that.

"John, I appreciate it, really I do."

He didn't believe that. She was still glaring at him.

"But you've gone overboard. And what is in all those boxes, for heaven's sake?"

"I don't know. Once they had your size, I told the salesladies to send a complete wardrobe. Whatever they thought you'd like."

"Good heavens! You mean you don't know how much you spent?"

"Rachel," he protested, exasperated. "I told you I have a lot of money. I can afford it."

"Then why are you still living in this neighborhood? I mean, it's not a bad neighborhood, but it's not like the Westers'."

He shrugged his shoulders. "I like it here. I've fixed up the house the way I want it. Why would I move? To have rich neighbors?"

"John, I—"

"Rachel, just put it all away and use it if you need it. It's just a uniform for the role you're playing. At the end of the year, if you don't want it anymore, you can give everything back to me."

"What would you do with it?"

"How the hell do I know? I said that so you'd quit fighting me," he admitted with a grin.

"*You* are a manipulator," she said, but she smiled in return and his heart lifted.

"I try," he agreed modestly.

She shook her head in mock disgust. "Okay, John, I'll use these things to play my role. But no more purchases, okay?"

"Okay."

She looked around her and then back at him. "I'm going to cook dinner now. At least that's something I can do. I can't cope with all this right now."

"Okay. But you'd better reassure Jacey on your way to the kitchen. Those tears really shook her up."

Concern about Jacey was the one subject that always got Rachel's attention. She hurried to Jacey's bedroom, next to hers, and closed the door behind her.

John wandered into his bedroom. It had certainly been an exciting day. More than he'd thought it would be. Panic had filled him at the wedding. Maybe that had been partly the cause of his massive purchases. His first wife had wanted only what he could buy her. Had he been throwing material things at Rachel because he was afraid he might offer more?

He was being ridiculous!

Their marriage was only temporary. Necessary for his business survival. That's all it was.

He stretched out on the bed and relaxed, having reassured himself. Faint noises came to his ears—Jacey playing in her room; Rachel in the kitchen. In a few minutes, an inviting smell floated up the stairs.

Hell, this marriage business, even on a temporary basis, might be a pretty good deal. He'd never felt more at home.

THEIR FIRST MEAL together had gone well, Rachel decided, entering her bedroom after tucking Jacey in for the night. She was pleasantly tired, ready for a good night's sleep.

The sight of her bed piled high with boxes made her groan. How could she have forgotten all those purchases? She'd accepted John's arguments because she really didn't have a choice. And he was right. She would have to dress the part of his wife, or the Westers wouldn't believe her.

Although she tried to suppress it, there was also a rising excitement at the thought of opening all those boxes. It was like Christmas without the wrappings. A Christmas like she'd never had before.

Making sure her door was closed, she approached the bed, a huge grin on her face. Since she'd agreed to this outrageous deal, she might as well enjoy it.

Starting at one corner, she opened a dozen pairs of shoes, both dressy and casual. Then she discovered handbags to accompany them. Another box contained several pairs of designer jeans. Sweatshirts and sweaters in various colors were there, too.

She began putting the clothes into the numerous drawers of the dresser. The furniture John had in this bedroom was cherry, highly polished and elegant. Fortunately, it also offered a lot of storage space.

When all those things were put away, she turned back to the bed, wondering what the other boxes could hold. A dozen pairs of expensive panty hose pleased her, although she wouldn't wear them to school. Her desk had rough edges and she frequently ruined her nylons. She would continue to use the grocery-store brands for teaching.

A new swimsuit surprised her. Her old one could be thrown out. The elastic in it had died last year. She held the new one up before the mirror. The legs were high-cut, French-style, giving her pause. Oh, well, as long as she was using John's pool—without John present. The thought of his gaze on her while she was wearing the swimsuit sent chills all over her body. She was going to have to watch herself. She reacted too strongly to John's masculine presence.

After all, he had no interest in her other than as a partner to save his company. There was nothing physical between them. John thought of her as his coconspirator.

That settled, she drew a deep breath and turned her attention back to the rest of the boxes.

The shock she felt when she discovered the contents of the next box was quickly replaced by incredible anger. Grabbing the item on top, she charged across the hall and burst into John's bedroom without knocking.

Chapter Eleven

Stretched out in bed, the *Wall Street Journal* in hand, John was congratulating himself on how well everything had worked out when his door was flung open.

He sat up in surprise as a wild-eyed Rachel marched to his bed, her hand extended in front of her. To his surprise, he realized she was dangling a black lace bra.

"John Crewes, how dare you?" she demanded in outraged tones.

"How dare I what?" he asked, unable to make any sense of her question. His mind immediately connected Rachel's heaving bosom with the article of clothing. Was it the wrong size?

"How dare you purchase this—this garment for me!"

"I did?"

"Well, of course you did! It was in the boxes you had delivered. You said you bought all of that for show. Surely you don't think I'm going to show my—my undergarments to anyone!"

He reached out to take the bra from her, looking from it to her chest. "If you do, you'll certainly get their attention."

She snatched it away from him. "How dare you!"

"You're repeating yourself, Rachel." When she looked as if she wanted to hit him, he raised a hand in surrender, but he couldn't hide his grin.

"Rachel, calm down. I didn't know they were going to include underwear. I swear, I didn't."

"Are you sure?" Even though her voice still held anger, he noticed her eyes widening as if she suddenly realized how she had acted. She moved a step back from the bed.

"I'm sure. But it looks like they made a nice choice." He smiled again, waving his hand toward the bra she still held.

Like a child, she hid the offending garment behind her back.

"Did they just send the one?" he asked calmly.

"I—I didn't count. You shouldn't have—I'll send them back tomorrow."

"Why? Don't you like them?" He craned his neck, as if to look behind her back, just to tease her.

She backed away. "That has nothing to do with it. You shouldn't be buying me underwear, even if you knew nothing about it."

"Don't go away, Rachel. I can't come after you without embarrassing us both."

"Why?" she asked, her eyes growing even more wary.

"Because I don't wear pajamas. Wait, Rachel!" he called, but she was already out the door, closing it behind her.

With a sigh, he slid from the bed and found a pair of gym shorts in one of the drawers. After putting them on, he crossed the hall to Rachel's room. Unlike her, he knocked and waited for an answer.

"Go away."

"Rachel, I just want to talk to you. Open up."

She finally opened the door, her gaze on the floor. "I'm sorry I didn't knock. Thank you for being so polite."

"Come on, Rachel, it's no big deal. At least, it isn't if you'll ever look at me again." He waited for her gaze to meet his. When she finally looked up, he grinned and she smiled briefly in return.

"That's better. Now, why did the, um, underwear upset you so much? We've argued this wardrobe thing to death. Surely we don't have to go over it again."

"It's too personal. I can buy my own underwear."

"Well, of course you can. But there's no reason why you should. I know we haven't worked out the details, but for the next year, you and Jacey are my family, and I'll provide for you—underwear, steaks, jelly beans, whatever."

"We don't eat steak all that often," she protested.

"See, there. I'll have lots of money left over for underwear," he teased.

"John, I appreciate your trying to make it less embarrassing, but I just want everything to be understood."

"Ah. You mean you're not offering to warm my bed as well as cook my dinner?" He admired the picture she made as her eyes widened at his frankness and her cheeks flooded with color. She was definitely a beauty.

She also didn't back down. "Exactly. I shouldn't have lost control and burst into your room, but—but I panicked. What we've done today has scared me just a little."

"It's scared me a lot, sweetheart. But that doesn't mean I'm going to take advantage of the situation. We made an agreement, and unless you want to modify it, we'll stick to our plans." His gaze dropped to the lace bra she still held in her hands. He had to crack down on his imagination as pictures of her modeling the garment floated before his eyes.

"Thank you. I won't bother you again," she muttered, her gaze shifting away from his.

He nodded, his mouth dry, and turned to leave the room. Pausing at the door, he added, "But I want you to know that I would be glad to have you warm my bed, should you change your mind."

She raised her chin and stared him right in the eye. "I won't."

"Darn. See you in the morning."

Although he closed the door behind him and returned to his empty bed and the *Wall Street Journal*, all he thought about until sleep claimed him was Rachel and a black lace bra. And then he dreamed about it.

JACEY AWOKE BEFORE HER mother called her for breakfast the next morning. She lay in the big bed, looking around her new room. The lion John had given her was standing guard at the end of her bed.

It was a nice room. It would look better when she brought more of her things from her house. But the nicest part about living in John's house was John. Now they were a real family. A mommy, a daddy, and a kid.

"Jacey, John, breakfast!" her mommy called. Jacey shoved back the sheet and climbed out of the bed. Breakfast was her favorite time of the day. And today she got to share it with John.

An hour later, she reached kindergarten and couldn't wait to talk to Lisbeth. She couldn't tell her that they'd just moved into John's house. Mommy had said that was a secret. But she could tell her about the lion and her new clothes.

After she shared her news with her best friend, she said with a satisfied sigh, "New daddies are the best."

"Yeah. My daddy is neat, too. Hey! We're going camping this weekend."

"Really?" Jacey replied with envy. "With your new daddy?"

"Yeah. And you're coming, too."

"I am? Did my mommy say?" Jacey knew she'd have to have her mother's approval.

"I think so. My mommy said we were all going together."

"Wow! That'd be so neat."

"Yeah. It's my daddy's plan."

"Daddies are neat."

"Yeah."

Contentment filled the air until Lisbeth spoke again. "There's just one thing about my new daddy I don't like."

"What?" Jacey asked in alarm. She couldn't think of anything she didn't like about John.

"I don't get to sleep with Mommy anymore. Used to, when I was scared, I could go get in her bed. Now Daddy's always there."

Jacey's heart beat faster. "Do all new mommies and daddies do that?"

"Sure. Don't yours?"

"Of course," Jacey said quickly. "I just wondered if maybe some didn't." She hoped Lisbeth believed her. She didn't want her friend to think anything was wrong.

"I think they all do. And they always kiss each other even when I'm around. It's disgusting!"

"Yeah. Disgusting."

Mrs. Wilson called the class to order and Jacey slid into her seat. But she didn't pay as close attention as she usually did. She had a lot to think about.

"JOHN? DAVID WESTER. Bud showed me the suggestions and projections you made. They are superb. Let's move ahead with your plans."

"No questions, David?" John asked, grinning into the telephone receiver, glad that his client couldn't see his reaction.

"None at all. You've sold Bud, and I can trust both of you."

"Great. I'll get started right away."

"Okay. Do you remember me asking you to hold your weekend open?"

"Sure. We're planning on going to the Charity Ball. Rachel bought a gown yesterday."

David laughed. "Carol's been shopping, too. But that's not what I've been planning for the weekend. I'm organizing a family camp-out. I want you and Rachel and Jacey to join us."

John didn't know what to say. He hadn't been camping in years and had no idea how Rachel felt about outdoor activities.

"Uh, I don't think we have any camping equipment," he said, hoping to postpone any commitment.

"We're providing everything, including the food. Just dress appropriately and come willing to work. It will be great fun. We'll leave about ten o'clock Saturday morning and come back Sunday evening. Meet at my house, okay?''

"Okay, sounds great to me." What else could he say? "Are you sure you don't want us to bring anything?"

"No, Carol's got it all arranged. We'll see you Friday evening."

"Right, Friday evening."

He hung up the phone and then stared at it. Could his life *get* any more complicated? His stomach had been tied in knots this morning facing Rachel over the breakfast table. After his interesting dreams of the night before, he could scarcely look her in the eye.

Now, he was facing a camping trip. And who knew how Rachel would react. With a sigh, he tried to rid his head of both David Wester's plans and Rachel. He found one easier to dismiss than the other. But work awaited. He had no choice.

"A CAMPING TRIP? Sweetie, I don't know anything about a camping trip," Rachel told Jacey as they drove home.

"Lisbeth said we were all going to go camping together this weekend. How long is it until the weekend?"

"Two more school days," Rachel said absentmindedly. She remembered David Wester asking them to hold their weekend open, but surely he would have said something to John by now, if he planned on them all camping together.

She sighed. That would be the last thing she needed. With only three weeks left of school, her students were turning in their term papers and she didn't have long to get them graded.

"Mommy?"

"Hmm?" Rachel answered distractedly.

"Does John kiss you?"

Rachel almost ran up on the curb. She straightened the car and quickly glanced down at Jacey's earnest face. "Let's wait just a minute until I stop the car, sweetie."

She pulled into her driveway and put the car into Park, then turned off the engine. "Now, what did you ask?"

"Does John kiss you?"

Rachel considered her answer. Clearly, this question was important to Jacey. Praying she was making the right choice, she said cautiously, "He has."

Jacey suddenly beamed at her. "Good." Then she undid her seat belt and opened the car door.

Rachel released the breath she'd been holding. Obviously she'd given the answer Jacey wanted. She hadn't added that she was going to be sure he never did again. But she was. She liked his kisses too much.

Rachel got out of the car, reaching into the back seat for her bag of term papers, then started up the sidewalk.

"Mommy!"

"Yes, sweetie?"

"You're going to the wrong house."

Screeching to a halt, Rachel looked longingly at her home before turning back to face her daughter. "Um, I think I forgot the key to John's house, Jacey."

"No, you didn't, Mommy. I watched John give you the key and you put it in your purse."

Her daughter was very good at remembering. "Oh, right. I'll have to look for it." Finding it just where

Jacey had said it would be, Rachel started walking over to John's house, reluctance filling her.

"Oh, Rachel!" a shrill voice called.

Recognizing Polly Meadows's voice, Rachel groaned. The woman was a dear, but the biggest gossip there was. "Hi, Polly," she said and kept walking.

"Are you visiting John? I don't think he's home."

Rachel was debating how much to tell the woman, when Jacey took the matter out of her hands.

"He's my new daddy. We live with him now."

Polly's reaction was shock. She dropped the hose she was using to water her roses, then screamed as cold water ran over the tops of her shoes.

"Lawsy me! Look what I've done." She snatched up the hose and then hurried over to turn off the water.

Rachel watched helplessly, knowing it would do her no good to run away. As soon as the water was turned off, Polly laid down the hose and came hurrying across the street. "What did that sweet child say?"

"John and I are married, Polly."

They hadn't discussed informing the neighbors, but Polly baby-sat for Rachel when she had to go out, and Rachel had planned on asking her to take care of Jacey Friday night. She had to know sometime.

"But he didn't even know where you were teaching just last week. When did the two of you meet?"

"A while back. We've kept things low-key because of—of Jacey, you know." She hoped Polly wouldn't question her deliberate vagueness.

"Of course, of course. Well, isn't that something? Does that mean you're moving out of your house?"

Reluctantly, Rachel nodded.

"'Cause a friend of mine has been looking for something on my street. It would be handy having her so close. I can't wait to tell her."

"I'm not sure yet when I'll be completely moved out. And I haven't notified the landlord yet. So I don't know when—"

"That's all right. She'll want to call them right away." Polly nodded her head and turned away. "My, my, my, what a surprise."

"Oh, Polly, I wondered if you could baby-sit for me Friday night? We have to go to the Charity Ball and—"

"The Charity Ball? That's a big social to-do. My, my, my, how quickly things change. Of course, I'll be happy to sit with little Jacey. Such a sweet child. Have you bought a dress, yet?"

"Yes, yesterday."

"I can't wait to see you all dressed up. You'll be as pretty as a picture! Now, I have to go call Beulah. She'll be so excited to hear about your house."

Rachel guessed she should be grateful for Beulah. Otherwise, Polly would have continued to ask questions for the next hour. But, somehow, she hadn't faced the fact that she wouldn't have her own house anymore. She'd even thought of continuing to pay the rent.

But that was absurd. She couldn't live next to John when their year was up. It would be too painful, for both her and Jacey. No, she might as well give up the house now and save all that rent money.

"Is Grandma Polly going to stay with me Friday night?" Jacey asked when Rachel reached John's front porch where the child had waited for her.

"Yes."

Since Rachel never saw her own parents, Polly Meadows had decided to adopt Jacey as her grand-daughter. Both Jacey and Polly seemed happy with the arrangement and Rachel had no real objection. Every child should have at least one grandparent.

"Open the door, Mommy. I got to go," Jacey said urgently, and Rachel followed her orders. Time to remember she was a mother.

IT WAS ALMOST SEVEN before John got home, even though he'd hurried through his work. He'd called Rachel and warned her of his tardiness.

Opening the door, he immediately smelled something good. He couldn't remember the last time he'd come home to a cooked meal waiting for him.

"Rachel?" he called, and Jacey burst through the kitchen door, racing to greet him.

"Well, hcllo, Jacey," he said, putting his briefcase on the floor and swinging her into his arms. The warm hug she gave him was sweeter than the biggest deal he'd ever made.

"Hi, Daddy," she replied, smacking him on the cheek.

It gave him a jolt, having her call him Daddy, but he decided he liked it.

"Jacey, I told you to ask John first."

"Oops, I forgot."

Rachel shook her head at her child.

"I don't mind," John assured her, smiling, hoping to receive a smile in return.

"She should've asked. Are you hungry? I saved dinner for you."

"I'm starved, but you don't have to cook for me, Rachel," he hurriedly added, although he was salivating over the thought of dinner.

"It's no trouble. Jacey and I have to eat, too."

He shed his jacket and tie and followed Rachel and Jacey into the kitchen. The breakfast table had a yellow tablecloth on it that he hadn't seen before.

"Is this new?"

"No. It's mine." Without saying anything else, she set down a plate full of steaming meat loaf, mashed potatoes and green beans, accompanied by several hot rolls. "Ice tea?"

"Yes. This looks wonderful, Rachel."

"It's just meat loaf."

"I love meat loaf. It's even better than a steak."

She recognized his teasing because the corners of her mouth tried to turn up, but she said nothing.

Before he could start to eat, Jacey pulled on his arm. "You forgot something."

"Oh, sorry, Jacey." He bowed his head to say a blessing, assuming that was Jacey's complaint.

"No, not that."

He looked down at the little girl even as Rachel protested.

"Jacey, of course John should—"

"Before that!" Jacey insisted.

"What did I forget, Jacey?"

"I kissed you hello, and you kissed me hello."

Distracted by Rachel and the enticing smell of his dinner, John wasn't following Jacey's line of reasoning. "Yeah?"

"Well, nobody kissed Mommy."

"Jacey!" Rachel objected again, much more vehemently, her cheeks bright red.

John stared at the two of them.

"I saw it on television," Jacey insisted. "When the daddy comes home, he kisses everybody."

"Um, I think you're right. A definite oversight."

"John!" Rachel protested and stepped back from the table.

"Rachel, we have to do the right thing," he said, keeping his voice calm and rational. Inside, anticipation was revving up his heartbeat.

"And Lisbeth said her mommy and daddy kiss all the time," Jacey added, her gaze darting between the two adults.

"Ah. Well, we want to do things like Lisbeth's mommy and daddy, don't we, Rachel?" He hoped she got the hint. If they were going to pull off this deal, they had to be thorough. And besides, he liked kissing her. A lot.

"Of—of course." Rachel didn't step away again, but she certainly wasn't rushing into his arms.

He rose from the table and went to her, taking her shoulders in his grasp. She raised one cheek toward him, but he wasn't about to settle for a peck. He covered her lips with his as Jacey clapped in the background.

Chapter Twelve

When John finally ended the kiss, leaving Rachel trembling, he didn't release her. In fact, he looked like he intended to repeat the gesture. In a panic, afraid she'd lose control completely if he did, Rachel pulled from his grasp.

"Your dinner will get cold."

"Dinner?" he repeated, as if in a fog.

"You were starving, remember?"

His gaze skimmed her body and that irresistible twinkle returned to his eyes. "Oh, yeah, I remember."

"John!" she chided, knowing he wasn't thinking of his meat loaf.

"Come on, Daddy. Mommy's meat loaf is good." Jacey tugged on his hand.

"I'm sure it is. Will you sit with me while I eat and tell me about your day?"

Jacey loved that idea and it gave Rachel some breathing room. She turned to the sink where she'd been rinsing their dinner dishes prior to putting them in the dishwasher.

"Camping? Oh, right, uh, Rachel," he called and she turned to look at him, a feeling of foreboding filling her.

"Yes?"

"David called today. He wants us to go camping with them this weekend."

"Yea!" Jacey cheered.

"Isn't this rather a surprise?"

"He did ask us to keep the weekend open."

"Yes, I know, but— Did you say yes?"

"What else could I say?" He shifted his gaze to Jacey and back again. "You understand?"

"Yes, of course," she agreed with a sigh. Everything they did seemed tied to the lie they were living. "We don't have a tent or anything. Do you?"

"David said not to worry. They'd provide everything, even food. We're just supposed to bring ourselves."

Rachel began mentally packing and making preparations. She'd bake oatmeal-raisin cookies. That would be a good snack for the kids. And she could buy some marshmallows for roasting. She could get most of her and Jacey's clothing in one bag.

"Maybe we'd better take my car. With bags and supplies, your car would be too crowded," she suggested.

John, his mouth full of his dinner, almost choked. Jacey leaned over and patted his back. He took a drink of tea and thanked her for her efforts.

"Um, Rachel, are you sure your car could make an out-of-town trip?"

She stiffened her spine. "My car may not be as luxurious as your Porsche, but it's in good running condition."

"Yeah, and only one window is stuck," Jacey chimed in.

John looked warily from her to Jacey and back again. "The air-conditioning does work, doesn't it?"

"We don't got none," Jacey said, smiling. "Mommy says we don't want to be all closed up when it's so pretty outside."

"Ah. I see. But on a long trip, it might be easier since we'll be going so fast. I think we could cram everything into my car."

"You want to take your car on a camping trip?" Rachel asked him, enjoying the look of dismay that filled him. "And let tree branches scrape the paint on it?"

"Hmm, I hadn't thought of that. How about I take your car in tomorrow for a thorough checkup before we drive it this weekend."

"My car is in good condition," she insisted huffily.

"Just to be sure, Rachel. Better safe than sorry," he added for good measure.

"I have to get to school. I can't do without a car."

"You can drive the Porsche."

She was amazed that he made the offer at all. After all, she knew how men were about their cars. But he said those words calmly, as if his offer was no big deal. She stared at him in surprise. "You've got to be kidding."

He looked at her and grinned. "Nope. Seems like the solution to me."

"But—but it's so expensive. What if I wrecked it, or one of my students damaged it?"

"Do they do that sort of thing?" he asked in surprise.

She turned her attention back to the sink. "It's been known to happen, if they get mad at you."

"Just don't make anyone mad tomorrow, okay?" he asked with another grin.

She rolled her eyes in exasperation. John turned his attention back to his dinner and her daughter. Rachel closed the dishwasher and then started making the cookies. It was a good thing she'd brought over the contents of her pantry last night, since John's had held only a few canned goods.

"What are you doing?" John asked, causing her to jump in surprise. He was standing right behind her, holding his empty plate.

"Making cookies. Did you want more dinner?"

"Nope. It was terrific. Need any help?"

She could tell he thought she'd refuse. "Thanks. If you'll just rinse your dishes and put them in the dishwasher, I'd appreciate it."

To his credit, he didn't blink an eye. "Yes, ma'am. My pleasure, ma'am."

"What's 'ma'am' mean?" Jacey asked, as usual standing next to John.

"You don't know what 'ma'am' means? Hasn't your mommy taken you to see any Westerns?" John asked in mock horror.

Jacey shook her head.

"What neglect! Your education has been sadly incomplete, my girl. Let's go in the den and discuss how we will rectify the matter."

Jacey stared at him, a puzzled frown on her face.

"He's teasing you, sweetie. Just humor him and take him out of the kitchen," Rachel ordered, smiling at her daughter.

RACHEL PULLED INTO John's driveway the next afternoon with a sigh of relief. She'd gotten the car home safely with no damage. In spite of John's casual attitude, she'd worried the entire day. Thank goodness she'd be back in her old, comfortable Chevrolet tomorrow.

Although her students would be disappointed. When one of her boys saw her pull into the teachers' parking lot in the Porsche, he'd raced over to examine the car. Then, of course, he'd immediately told all his friends, although she'd assured him it wasn't her car. She'd been the star attraction most of the day.

She and Jacey had just reached the porch, after carefully collecting any minute scrap of paper they might have dropped in the Porsche, when a brand-new green Volvo station wagon pulled into the driveway. As John got out of the driver's seat, Rachel walked toward him slowly, her mind examining the evidence.

"Where's my car?"

"Well, I got to thinking, Rachel. I didn't want you driving something that might break down at any moment, and a station wagon would give us all a lot more room."

When she didn't answer, and only continued to frown at him, he added, "It has air-conditioning."

"Where's my car?" she repeated.

"I traded it in," he finally admitted, that sideways grin on his face.

"How can you do that? The car is in my name."

"I told them you'd come down this evening and sign the title over to them." He held up his hands as she advanced toward him. "I know I shouldn't have done it without your approval, but I was sure you wouldn't agree. It's the only sensible thing to do, Rachel. Honest.''

"Sensible? Sensible! How could you, John?" She glared at both him and the car as if they were monsters.

"Look, Rachel, we're putting it in your name. It's paid for. When the year—" He broke off, staring at Jacey before bringing his gaze back to Rachel. "It will be yours, no strings attached."

She stared at him in bewilderment and despair. It seemed impossible to stop him from making these expensive offerings. She didn't know what to do.

"John, you can't— This is totally unnecessary."

"That's not true, Rachel. It is necessary. You and Jacey could break down on the highway. That's dangerous. I can afford to provide you with a reliable car. It's not like I bought you a Cadillac or a Mercedes."

She gasped. Surely he wouldn't have— She saw in his gaze that he'd considered it. Closing her eyes, she prayed for guidance. This man was impossible.

"You mean it's ours?" Jacey suddenly asked, touching the car with one finger.

"That's right, sweetheart. Want to get inside?" He swung open the door and Jacey cautiously climbed in. After all the rules her mother had given her about riding in the Porsche, she knew how to treat an expensive vehicle.

"Mommy, it smells new," Jacey said reverently, as if she were experienced in such things.

"Rachel?" John asked, indicating the driver's seat.

"Mommy, aren't you going to say thank-you?" Jacey prompted, leaning out the back door to watch.

"Yes, of course," Rachel said stiffly, avoiding John's gaze. "Thank you."

"Don't you want to try it out?"

"Not now. I have to get the title from—from my house." She backed away from John's latest extravagance, as if afraid to get too close.

"Mommy, you didn't kiss John to say thank-you."

John must have read the panic in her eyes, or he wasn't interested in that kind of gratitude, either. He touched Jacey's shoulder and said, "Later, Jacey. Your mom wants to thank me later."

Much later. Maybe next year. Maybe never.

JOHN EASED THE COLLAR of his tuxedo shirt as he stood in the hallway, outside Rachel's door. Somehow, he didn't think she was going to appreciate his next move. His ex-wife had not only wanted gifts, she'd insisted he buy her anything she wanted. And he hadn't made a fortune then.

Rachel, on the other hand, made him feel like a villain because he bought her things. He looked down at the black velvet box in his hands. He was going to be truly evil this evening, in that case.

He raised his fist to tap on the door just as Rachel opened it. She jumped back, her beautiful lips shaped in a surprised *O* that made him yearn to touch them.

"You surprised me," she said, a hesitant smile on her face. "Are you ready to go?"

"Almost." He took a step back to take in Rachel in all her glory. She was magnificent. The blue of her eyes matched her gown. "Uh, before we go, I bought you something to go with the dress."

A wary look came into her eyes. "What?"

He'd automatically hidden the box behind his back when she'd opened the door. Before he showed her, he decided to do a little advance work. "Rachel, all the women tonight are going to be wearing jewels."

"I'm sure there will be many who won't have jewels, John. You're exaggerating. Besides, I don't have any." Her chin came up, as if he were impugning her honor.

John shrugged and grinned, bringing his hand forward. "Yes, you do."

She looked at velvet box and then up at him. As if he hadn't spoken, hadn't offered her the box, she swept up her long skirt and headed toward the stairs.

"Rachel! Where are you going?"

She ignored him.

He raced after her, grasping her arm just before she started downstairs. Although he pulled her to a halt, she refused to face him.

"Won't you even look at it?" he pleaded.

"No."

"Why not? You might like it."

Now she turned to him and pushed against his chest with both hands. "Of course, I might like it! Do you think I don't like new clothes, new cars, new everything? Do you really think I'm that odd?"

"Rachel—"

"You think I prefer beat-up old cars that have oil leaks and always break down? That I like to make my own clothes and teach summer school?" She continued to push him back, fire in her eyes.

"Rachel—"

"Maybe you think I like being alone, staying home, never going out. You probably think I'm an old fuddy-duddy who's no fun at all!"

John couldn't hold back a chuckle and his arms came around her slim curves. "Yeah. I think you're an old fuddy-duddy, the sexiest old fuddy-duddy I've ever seen." Before she could protest again, his lips covered hers. He loved the softness of her. The taste of her. Her.

He jerked back from her as he realized what had just passed through his head. No. No, he didn't love her. He was just turned on by a sexy lady.

"Here," he said, thrusting the box into her hand. "Put this on and wear it. If you don't want it after tonight, you can sell it, or give it back, or throw it away. But tonight, you have to look like your husband is successful, okay?"

He charged past her down the stairs, hoping to run away from his dangerous thoughts.

RACHEL HURRIED DOWN the stairs, belying her weariness. She wasn't used to such late nights. They'd gotten home about one-thirty in the morning.

While John had walked Polly across the street, Rachel had quickly removed the sapphire-and-diamond pendant he had given her earlier, put it back in its little velvet box and left it on the dresser in John's room.

If she hadn't given it back last night, she might have kept it forever. It was beautiful. But she couldn't keep it. Although John had given her a searching look this morning over breakfast, he'd said nothing.

"Ready, Rachel?" he called from the bottom of the stairs.

"Yes. What are you eating?" Her gaze traveled from him to Jacey, standing just behind him. "Jacey? Are you eating something, too?"

"I told you she'd catch us," Jacey said accusingly.

"Did you get into the cookies?"

"It's my fault, Rachel. They looked too good to pass up." John ducked his head as if he were ashamed.

"You can't fool me, mister. You're not sorry," she claimed in disgust. "It's nine-thirty. You just finished breakfast half an hour ago."

"We just had one, Mommy," Jacey chirped as she slipped her hand into John's.

Rachel couldn't hold back a grin any longer. "Okay, okay, since it was just one. But no more cookies at least until we get out of the driveway."

They both grinned at her leniency and headed for the door.

She sighed. John and Jacey were such friends already. Rachel worried about her child's disappointment when the year ended.

She joined them outside, where John was standing by the Volvo, although Jacey was already in the back seat.

"Do you want me to drive, or shall you?" he asked.

She appreciated the sensitivity of his question. After all, he'd made a point of putting the car in her name. She tossed him her keys. "You drive. I'm going to relax. I'm not used to late nights."

"But you had fun?"

"Yes, I did, which was a surprise."

"You thought everyone would be stuffy and no fun, didn't you? Maybe a bunch of fuddy-duddies?"

There was that blasted twinkle in his eyes again as he teased her. "Maybe that's why I enjoyed myself. I felt at home."

He burst out laughing and she stuck out her tongue, feeling like a kid again.

"What's so funny?" Jacey called from inside the station wagon. She already had her seat belt on, ready for their trip.

"Nothing, sweetie," Rachel assured her. How could she explain the pleasure she got from John's teasing? Or the relief she'd felt last night when she'd discovered she fit in with the people attending the Charity Ball. She didn't even want to try.

"Did you put the bag in the back?" she asked John.

"Uh, sort of."

They were each getting ready to slide into the car and she looked at him over its roof. "Now what?"

"I repacked everything into one bag."

She stared at him and then ducked down to look into the back of the station wagon. Instead of the beat-up duffel she'd packed, there was only a black leather bag, slightly larger. Popping back up, she demanded, "Why did you do that?"

"Because," he explained softly, "I thought it would look kind of strange for our things to be in different bags. Like we hadn't packed together."

Her cheeks reddened as she thought of the personal items he'd handled. "You should have let me repack everything."

"Not a chance. I didn't want you handling my underwear," he said primly, his nose in the air, but with that twinkle back in his eyes.

"John Crewes, I am definitely going to wring your neck as soon as I get you alone."

His grin spread. "I can't wait, Rachel Crewes. I just can't wait."

Chapter Thirteen

Other than Jacey's occasional comments or questions, they rode in silence until they were out of Kansas City. They were going to Perry Lake, only about an hour away. John watched Rachel out of the corner of his eye, enjoying her relaxed companionship.

"Oh, by the way," he said, suddenly remembering, "when I walked Polly home last night, she wanted to know how soon you'd be moved out of your house. She's got a friend who wants to rent it."

Rachel's body tensed, and she frowned. "I know. She mentioned it."

When she said nothing else, he prompted, "Well?"

"I don't know."

"I thought you were going to save your rent money for—well, for later?"

"I am."

"Then, the sooner you vacate, the better it will be for you," he reasoned.

"Thanks for that exercise in logic," she murmured, her face turned away.

"Rachel—"

"Just leave it, John. I'll take care of it."

Her attitude made him think more closely about how the move must be affecting her. She was probably having difficulty letting go of her home. If she wanted to keep it, he supposed he didn't mind, but it was senseless to pay rent when she didn't have to.

A sudden thought struck him. He glanced sideways at Rachel, as if to be sure she hadn't noticed anything, but she was still staring out the window. She'd refuse, of course, but he could do it without her approval. He'd just buy the house, put it in her name, and then lease it to Polly's friend. Not only would Rachel not have to pay rent, but she'd also get income from the house.

Then, when their year was over, she and Jacey would still be close enough for him to take care of them, watch over them. He already knew how lonesome he'd be when they moved out of his house. Four days, and he didn't want to go back to living alone.

It wasn't just the food Rachel cooked, although she was great in the kitchen. It wasn't just the companionship they shared, including Jacey. It wasn't even Jacey's smiles and hugs, which were warm enough to heat a house in winter. He couldn't even say it was the sexual tension that hummed between him and Rachel at certain moments. It was a combination of all those things.

After years of being alone, concentrating on work, he felt as if he'd broken out into the sunshine. His senses were heightened, his gaze sharpened, his body tightened to a new intensity that stimulated him to greater heights.

"Are we almost there?" Jacey asked from the back seat.

John automatically looked at Rachel as she turned, and their smiles met. He fought the sudden urge to pull over to the side of the road and kiss her senseless.

"Not yet, Jacey. It will only be about fifteen more minutes," Rachel answered.

"Can you tell time?" John asked, wondering why he hadn't thought of that question before.

"A'course," Jacey said indignantly. "I'm not a baby."

"But you don't have a watch."

"Mommy said maybe at Christmas," Jacey assured him.

"I could—"

"John!" Rachel snapped. "Don't even think about it."

"But, Rachel—"

"John, you can't keep buying us things."

Damn. He'd upset her again. And if she rejected the idea of his buying her daughter a cheap watch, how was she going to feel about his buying her a house? He already knew the answer to that question.

Squaring his jaw, he focused on the road ahead of him, but inside he was plotting. Rachel deserved the best. He owed her. And he was going to pay her for her sacrifice. One way or another.

When they pulled into the campground behind David Wester's minivan, Jacey was anxious to be released from the station wagon. Rachel gave her permission to find Lisbeth, and she and John stood beside their car to watch the happy reunion between the two little girls.

"You'd think they'd been apart for years," he murmured.

"It probably seemed like it to them."

John let his gaze leave the children to look at the people emerging from the other vehicles. "Six couples and a lot of kids. I wonder what David has in mind?"

"And one of them is very pregnant. I don't think she should be so far from a hospital," Rachel added, staring at a young woman just getting out of a sedan.

John noted the soon-to-be new mother and privately agreed with Rachel. He hoped there would be no emergencies. He knew nothing about childbirth.

"Were you ever that big with Jacey?" he asked, fascinated by the pregnant woman.

Rachel groaned. "I thought I was as big as a Volkswagen. Now, I'm not sure."

"And you were all alone?"

"Yes," was her clipped reply, and she pressed her lips tightly together.

He couldn't resist putting his arm around her shoulders. "I didn't mean to bring up bad times."

Much to his surprise, she relaxed in his embrace. "They weren't, really. At least, in the end they weren't. Jacey is the center of my universe."

"I can understand that," he replied, leaning over to kiss her forehead.

"That's what I like to see," David boomed behind them, jolting them both.

"What's that?" John asked, dropping his arm from Rachel's shoulders.

"Affection. Touching. All those good things. I firmly believe it's the little things that make a marriage work."

"Now, David, don't start lecturing," Carol Wester teased, coming up behind her husband. "You and John need to organize a tent-raising crew, while we women get started on lunch. Those kids are going to be hungry before you know it.''

David led John away and Carol took Rachel over to introduce her to the other women. The children were sent to bring in firewood while the women got out the fixings for hamburgers.

Rachel watched the men set up the tents in a large circle around the campfire. With all the changes in her life the past week, somehow she hadn't considered the sleeping arrangements on this camping trip. She felt a little stunned by her obtuseness.

"How many tents will there be?" she asked, as casually as possible.

"I believe David planned on eight. One for each of the families, and then one for the older boys and one for the older girls," Carol told them. She turned to the other ladies. "Sarah, you have three kids, don't you, and Mary, you have four, and, of course, the one on the way."

"Yes," Mary said, pausing to rub her back. "And if this one doesn't come soon, I'm going to give up. I feel like I've been pregnant forever."

All the women nodded in understanding.

"The other two still have little children," Carol continued, "so we thought everyone could keep their little ones with them."

Rachel breathed a sigh of relief. "Good idea. Jacey wouldn't want to be with a group of strange kids." Even if she wanted to, Rachel wasn't about to permit it. She needed her daughter as a buffer between her and John.

"You'll also be glad to know we have air mattresses for everyone," Carol added with a chuckle. "David likes to go first-class."

Rachel certainly couldn't complain about the provisions the Westers had made for their convenience. Lunch was delicious and the cleanup relatively easy. David then asked the older children to escort the younger ones to the playground nearby while he talked with their parents.

Wondering what was coming next, Rachel shot a concerned look at John. He interpreted her worry as a mother's fear for her child's safety. "Jacey will be fine. We can see the playground from here," he assured her.

"Do you know what David wants to discuss?" she whispered.

"No, but it's probably nothing to worry about."

Easy for him to say, she thought, then wondered why it would be any easier for John. Jacey, of course. She was the added dimension that made it more difficult for Rachel. Except that John always considered Jacey. Rachel could give him credit for that.

"Everyone have a seat," David invited, gesturing to the camp chairs he'd provided.

John chose a flat rock near the campfire and pulled Rachel down beside him. When he draped his arm across her shoulders, she stared up at him, and he whispered in response to her unspoken question, "For show."

Since he added a kiss on her neck before turning his face back toward David, Rachel wasn't sure she believed him. He loved to tease her.

"The reason I asked you all to come camping with us this weekend is because I'm starting a new project, and I'd like your help." David paused to look at each couple. "I've seen all of you interact as a family, and I've been impressed with the love and happiness displayed there. What you may not know about each other, since most of you are strangers, is that every family here today is a blended family.''

The couples all looked around at each other, smiling acknowledgment of their situations.

''As you know, I only recently joined your group, though I'm not the most recent newlywed. John and Rachel carry that honor. But I'm aware of how many couples in America are going or have gone through the adjustment period resulting from the mixing of two families. I want my next video to deal with that subject. And I want your help.''

Rachel thought she was going to die.

JACEY AND LISBETH climbed the jungle gym on the playground.

''This is fun,'' Jacey said. ''I'm glad you invited us.''

''Me, too!'' Lisbeth agreed with a giggle.

''Sleeping in a tent is going to be fun. I've never done that before.''

''Yeah. But I'm glad I get to sleep with my mommy and daddy. It's a little scary.''

''Do you all sleep in the same bed?'' She remembered Lisbeth's earlier complaint.

''No. I get a sleeping bag by myself. Mommy and Daddy share the big one.''

Jacey nibbled on her bottom lip. Was that what would happen in her tent? Would she see her mommy and John in the big sleeping bag? Somehow, she didn't think so. She thought her mommy would make John take the sleeping bag by himself. After all, they didn't share the same room at home.

She looked at her friend and then back toward the campfire where the parents were all sitting. "I wish we could spend the night together," she said, watching Lisbeth closely.

"Yeah! That'd be fun."

They swung down from the bars and then climbed them again. "We could tell each other stories to help us sleep," Jacey said wistfully.

"Yeah. And I've got my own flashlight," Lisbeth bragged.

"I don't have one."

"You need one at night. There's no bathroom in the tent," Lisbeth explained with a giggle. "But I could share with you if we were in the same tent."

"That'd be neat."

"I know!" Lisbeth squealed.

"What?"

"Let's ask my mommy if you can move your sleeping bag into my tent."

"Do you think she'd let me?"

"Sure. And we can ask your mommy, too."

"Let's ask your mommy first, and then she can ask my mommy. That would be best."

"Okay."

Yeah, that would be best. Because Jacey didn't think her mommy was going to like the idea. She didn't want to make her mommy or John angry. She just wanted them to be a family.

WHEN THEY TOOK A break from their discussions, Rachel carried the bag John had packed to the tent Carol had designated as theirs. She breathed a sigh of relief when she noted the double sleeping bag and the single laid out on the other side.

Close quarters might be a little difficult, but John was a gentleman. He would take the single and she and Jacey the double. With their tent flap zipped, no one would know the difference.

She pushed the bag to the back of the tent and sat down on the double sleeping bag. The air mattress was wonderful. She considered stretching out for a nap. Her late night and the tension of the day was catching up with her. David had asked that they have another discussion group before dinner.

She'd kept quiet most of the time this afternoon. After all, as the newest blended family, they weren't exactly the voice of experience. What an understatement. They weren't even a blended family. A marriage license didn't make them a family.

"Daddy!"

Jacey's voice sounded across the campground, and Rachel moaned. Jacey didn't need a marriage license to adopt John Crewes. She had been enthusiastic from the start.

"Rachel?"

John's voice sounded just outside the tent. "Yes, John, come on in."

"Everything okay?"

"Just fine," she assured him as he ducked into the tent. "I was just considering a nap."

"And I was just considering an oatmeal-raisin cookie. Got any left?" He looked around the small area.

"There were plenty left a few minutes ago. They're outside, on the picnic table."

"Damn. I'll bet those blasted kids have inhaled them."

"John! You're supposed to be a loving father, remember?" she protested, unable to resist teasing him.

"I love Jacey. I don't have to love those other kids. They're going to eat all my cookies."

"Daddy, Mommy!" Jacey called and then pulled back the tent flap. "Hi."

"Hi, sweetheart. Did you have fun?" John asked.

"Yeah, this is great!"

"Do you want to lie down on your bed and rest awhile?" Rachel asked, although she was sure she knew the answer. Jacey considered herself much too old for naps.

"No! Where are the cookies? Me and Lisbeth wanted a snack."

"They're on the picnic table. Mrs. Wester has something for you to drink, too."

Before Jacey could run off, John stopped her. "Jacey, bring me some cookies, okay? And a soda would be nice, too."

"Okay," she agreed and disappeared.

"I think she's having a good time," John said, satisfaction in his voice.

"Of course, she is."

"Are you?"

Rachel leaned back on the sleeping bag, propping her head up with one hand. "It's not bad."

"They seem like nice people."

"Yes, they do. Especially Mary."

"Yeah. She gets a lot done for someone as pregnant as she is." John moved to the edge of the sleeping bag, shifting Rachel's legs over as he sat down.

She pulled herself away from his touch, making sure there was plenty of room between them. "I thought you'd sleep on the single mattress and Jacey and I would take this one," she hurriedly explained.

"Yeah, I figured," he assured her, that twinkle in his eye.

Rachel was embarrassed and said nothing. John seemed content to sit silently. It was a pleasantly cool afternoon, but the shade of the tent was welcome.

"When you were pregnant with Jacey, did she kick a lot?"

"All the time," Rachel complained, although she smiled. "I thought for sure I had a little boy, a future soccer star."

"Girls can play soccer."

"I know. I started to sign Jacey up for it this spring, but I thought we'd wait until next year."

"Why?"

"It's difficult to get her to practice because of my job."

"Oh. Does she take dance lessons, or piano lessons?"

"No." She didn't want to add that she couldn't afford lessons. After she taught school this summer and used the extra income to pay off her college loans, then she could provide her child with lessons.

"Would you want to stay home with Jacey instead of teaching?"

Rachel started to dismiss his question. She didn't want to get to know John better, or for him to know her. She was too attracted to him as it was. But the sincerity in his gaze wouldn't allow her to ignore his interest.

"No. Jacey's not home all day now. Next year, she'll be at school almost as long as I am. I wouldn't mind teaching part-time, maybe just the mornings."

She shrugged. "That's a ridiculous thought, because teachers never get ahead financially. I'll always be teaching, until I'm old and gray and have to retire."

"This next year, you could—"

"No, John. Don't even start. This next year, we're going to continue as we always have. That's the best way."

"I'm not sure—"

"Rachel? Are you in there?"

"Yes, Carol. Come in." It sounded ridiculous to be so formal in a canvas tent.

The tent flap was pulled back and Carol ducked her head in. "You sure it's all right?"

"Of course. We were just talking," John assured her. "I can leave if you need to talk to Rachel alone."

Without thinking, Rachel grabbed the back belt-loop of his jeans. She wasn't about to be abandoned by that rat!

"No, that's not necessary. In fact, you'll probably both like what I have to say," Carol said with a smile that suggested naughty things.

John's eyebrows rose as he looked first at Carol and then at Rachel.

Blushing, Rachel sat up, letting go of John's jeans.

"Our two little darlings have come up with a plan," Carol explained. "They thought tonight would be a lot more fun if they got to sleep in the same tent."

Rachel worked to hide her dismay. Then she hurriedly tried to make the best of things. "Of course. We'll be happy to have Lisbeth stay with us."

"No, no, Jacey must come to our tent. You see, we have the largest tent. David said it's a perk he deserves because Lisbeth and I bring so much stuff," Carol explained with a chuckle. "There wouldn't be room to bring another sleeping bag and air mattress into your tent.''

Rachel looked at the space around her and knew Carol was right. But she didn't want to admit it. ''Couldn't the girls sleep in the same sleeping bag?''

''Oh, they'd never get to sleep that way. In separate bags, I'm hoping they'll drift off by midnight. And, in the meantime, that will give you and John a night without kids. I know she's in a different room at home, but you don't even have to worry about her tonight. I'll take good care of her.''

Assuming they were in agreement, Carol backed out of the tent. Just as she was lowering the tent flap, she added, ''And you two can do whatever you want.''

Dead silence followed Carol's departure.

''Does she think we're going to have an orgy in a canvas tent with neighbors five feet on either side of us?'' Rachel finally demanded, her voice tight with tension.

''I'm game if you are,'' John told her, a grin on his lips.

Chapter Fourteen

"John Crewes!" Rachel protested.

"Hey, I only offered to cooperate. You were the one grabbing hold of me, not the other way around."

"I didn't want you to abandon me to—"

"Knock, knock!" David called from outside the tent.

John rolled his eyes at Rachel even as he called out for David to come in.

"Shoot, John, if I'd known you were in here," David said as he lifted the tent flap, "I would've told Carol to make *you* move Jacey's bed."

Move Jacey's bed.

Rachel sat in frozen silence as the two men joked over the chore. Somehow, in the brief minutes since Carol's departure, Rachel hadn't realized exactly how much Jacey's arrangement would affect her and John. But when David, with John's help, rolled up the single sleeping bag and took it and the air mattress from the tent, the result was obvious.

She and John were supposed to sleep in the double sleeping bag—together.

Sharing a tent with John presented difficulties, but there was still enough space to avoid touching each other. Sharing a sleeping bag was a different matter.

She couldn't do it. She simply couldn't align her body with John's and go to sleep. A brief whimper escaped as she considered the torture of lying next to him in the darkness.

She'd been a naive girl when she'd met Dirk, Jacey's eventual father. He'd been experienced, sexy, determined to seduce her. And he'd done so with relative ease, much to her embarrassment afterward. But his kisses, his touch, weren't even on the same chart with John Crewes's.

Even understanding her sexual nature now, and taking all precautions to resist him, Rachel melted when John kissed her. Against all her self-admonitions, she simply melted.

And now she was going to spend the entire night in the same sleeping bag with him?

Maybe the relative closeness of their neighbors would save her. Or maybe John wouldn't kiss her. Or have any interest in touching her. Maybe.

John raised the tent flap and entered the tent again. Rachel looked away. She couldn't meet his gaze. He might realize how panic-stricken she was.

She felt the air mattress shift as he settled down beside her again, but still she didn't look at him.

"Want a cookie?"

Such a mundane offer was a ridiculous contrast to her steamy thoughts and she turned to stare at him. With a grin, he held out one of her oatmeal-raisin cookies. "I snagged a few on the way back."

He also offered one of the cans of soda he had tucked under his arm. "I thought a little sugar might lessen the shock of sleeping with me."

She glared at him even as she took both. "I suppose it won't bother you at all!"

"Oh, it'll bother me, Rachel," he drawled. "A lot."

"Then why didn't you say something? I didn't realize—"

"Neither did I, until David arrived. By then, it was too late. What reason would I have given for changing our minds? We didn't trust them to take care of Jacey?"

She knew he couldn't have said that. Truthfully, in all the time since his and David's departure, she hadn't been able to come up with an excuse. It was unfair of her to expect him to have done so in a lot less time. "I know. But what are we going to do?"

He took a long sip of his soda, tipping his head back, and she was tempted to stroke his exposed skin. With a gasp, she drew back even farther from him.

"I suspect we'll sleep on this air mattress."

"I have another solution," she said, hoping for a different outcome. "I'll give you the sleeping bag and you can sleep over there." She gestured to the empty side of the tent.

"Nope."

"John, we can't—we can't share this sleeping bag."

"That sounds better than waking up tomorrow morning a cripple. I'm too old to sleep on this hard, rocky ground."

It was hard. They hadn't worried about seeking out grassy knolls or rock-free areas because they had the air mattresses. But she would do what she had to do.

"Then I'll take the sleeping bag."

"Rachel, I can't let you do that. You wouldn't get any sleep and you'd be miserable the rest of the trip."

"No, I wouldn't."

"You remind me of Jacey. She gets that stubborn look just like you."

"I'm not being childish," she told him. "I'm just trying to prevent anything from happening."

"Rachel, as you so wisely pointed out, this is a canvas tent and we have neighbors on both sides. We're just going to sleep side by side, not have an orgy."

She didn't respond. How could she? Her mind was taken up with the mental picture of an orgy with only the two of them.

"Come on, let's go for a walk. We'll take Jacey and Lisbeth with us." He set aside his snack, stood, half bent-over, and offered a hand to Rachel.

She traded the soda and cookie for his hand without hesitation. She was all for getting out of the tent. By the time morning rolled around, she suspected she'd hate those four canvas walls.

THE REST OF THE DAY passed with relative pleasure— as long as Rachel didn't think about the night to come. They had hiked along the edge of the lake with the girls. John had shown infinite patience, pointing out things of interest and answering the millions of questions children ask.

Dinner preparation had given Rachel a respite from his continuous presence, but, perversely, she missed him, and her gaze kept straying to the game of horseshoes the men were playing. When their eyes met, she would quickly turn away, pretending some urgency in the task at hand.

After dinner, David asked them all, as a group, to discuss the difficulties they'd faced as they became families. John gathered Jacey into his lap and clasped Rachel's hand in his.

Rachel ignored the discussion going on around her. She watched her daughter and John. Jacey's ponytail bounced with her every move, brushing John's jaw. Occasionally he'd lean forward and place a kiss on her forehead, or she'd rest her head against his broad chest. Once, she leaned back and patted his cheek with her hand, whispering something Rachel couldn't hear.

"What did you want to say, Jacey?" David asked.

Concerned, Rachel leaned forward, but John squeezed her hand, telling her to trust Jacey.

"My daddy talks to me," Jacey announced, as if she'd said something of great import. "He asks me to sit with him while he eats his dinner and tell him about school and things."

"Like Mr. Sam?" David asked, smiling gently.

"Yeah, and he 'members."

"You're right, Jacey. That's very special." David nodded in approval at John.

David was right. It was special that John took the time to listen to Jacey. And he didn't do that to impress David. He hadn't known David would find out whether he took the time for Jacey. It was just something that came naturally to John.

It was a real shame that he wasn't a father to a dozen kids. Rachel thought he would be perfect. When their year was past, perhaps he would find a woman to love and have a family with. She wanted John to be happy. But her stomach hurt at the thought.

Too soon, in Rachel's opinion, the small children went to bed. She helped Jacey settle in the Westers' tent with Lisbeth, amid much giggling. When Rachel returned to the campfire, John had moved back to the big rock they'd sat on at lunch, and he pulled her down to sit between his legs, her back against his chest. His arms encircled her and she found herself gently cradled.

That was another amazing factor she hadn't expected in John Crewes. His gentleness. She'd expected a hardened man, bitter, thinking only of himself. Instead, John had been patient, teasing, kind. His love for Jacey seemed unending, and he was sensitive to Rachel's feelings before she even recognized them herself.

"Rachel, you haven't said much," David observed, looking at her over the campfire.

"We haven't been married all that long," she replied with a shrug, hoping no one guessed just how short their marriage really was. "I think we're still in the honeymoon phase."

"And loving it," John assured their audience. She looked up in time to see him wiggle his eyebrows suggestively.

Talk continued for another couple of hours, but Rachel said nothing else. How could she? Her senses were engaged in warfare. John's touch encouraged abandonment of all self-discipline. She fought giving in.

Close to eleven, John whispered, "Ready for bed?"

The low, seductive timbre of his voice sent shivers all over her, and Rachel shifted uneasily. "Uh, no, I'm not sleepy at all."

"Liar," John accused with a chuckle. "You've been yawning for the past half hour."

"Just nerves," she whispered tersely.

"Well," David said with a stretch, "I think Carol and I will turn in. After all, we have dual alarm clocks in our tent in the persons of Jacey and Lisbeth. John, we'll keep an eye on Jacey in the morning if you two want to sleep past dawn."

"Thanks, David. I'll owe you one."

John's arms disappeared from around her and his rock-hard chest no longer supported her. Before she could adjust to the change, he was in front of her, offering a hand to help her stand.

"Come on, Sleeping Beauty. Time for bed."

Since there was a general exodus and one of the men was smothering the campfire, Rachel could think of no excuse to postpone the inevitable. She groaned as she stood. "That rock needs a cushion."

"I'll give you a massage," he offered with a grin.

"No, thank you."

"Your loss. Come on, I'll walk you to the facilities, since we only have one flashlight."

When they finally headed for their tent, most of the camp had settled in for the night. There were murmurs of voices rising from various tents, but otherwise, the silence of the forest fell around them.

"Look at all the stars," John said, catching her arm before she could duck into the tent. He'd turned off the flashlight, making it easier to look heavenward.

She straightened and looked up, admiring the beauty of the night, and his arms came around her, as they had done while they were seated on the rock. Tensing, she tried to pull away.

"Relax, Rachel. I'm just keeping you warm."

"Much warmer, and I'll go off like a Roman candle," she muttered and then regretted her words.

"You, too?"

"Why do you continue to—to touch me if you know what it's doing to us?" she whispered fiercely.

"I can't help myself," he murmured before turning her around and kissing her.

The white-hot heat of the brightest star seemed mild compared to Rachel's response to his kiss. All evening he had caressed her, cradled her, making her want more and more of his touch. She met his embrace as if they were long-lost lovers.

"You two need to get inside your tent before the teenagers see you and get ideas," Mary's husband suggested with a laugh as he walked past them.

"Right," John responded huskily.

Rachel buried her face in his chest, embarrassed to have been observed in her surrender to John's sexy kiss.

"Come on, sweetheart," he whispered, pulling her after him into the tent.

When he would have continued their embrace once they were inside, she backed away from him.

"No, John. We can't. Everyone else may think our marriage is real, but we both know it's not." She reached the far side of the tent, an entire five feet away, and stopped, holding her breath.

"That marriage license looked pretty real to me," he growled.

"The license may be real, but the marriage isn't. I let my hormones rule my head once. I won't do it again." She hoped she sounded more confident that she felt. Her knees were shaking. If he ignored her protest and took her back into his arms, she'd be lost.

"Get ready for bed," he ordered in clipped tones and turned and left the tent.

After the first shocked moment, Rachel didn't waste any time. She changed from jeans to jogging shorts and a T-shirt. Then she pulled the sleeping bag from the air mattress and took it to the other side of the tent. At least she had her own pillow from home. Her head would probably be the only part of her body that wouldn't ache in the morning.

By the time John returned, she'd settled into her new bed, her back turned to the tent entrance. Even so, she knew at once when John stepped inside.

With the flashlight left sitting on the air mattress so he wouldn't have any trouble locating his things, he also wouldn't have any difficulty understanding what she'd done. Jacey had insisted on toting along a beach towel, in case it was warm enough to swim the next day, and Rachel had spread it out on the air mattress for John.

There was a moment after his entrance when he didn't move, and Rachel tensed, waiting for his reaction. Then he moved to the back of the tent where she'd left the bag. The sound of his zipper being lowered was almost more than she could bear as her imagination ran wild. She heard the denim brush against his flesh with agonizing slowness as he removed his jeans.

Rachel covered her ears beneath the cloth of the sleeping bag, trying to avoid the sounds that aroused her imagination. It was going to be hard enough to sleep on the rocky ground without hearing every breath John took.

Even so, she kept waiting for him to lie down on the air mattress. Suddenly, she was swung up into the air, sleeping bag and all. Her gasp was shushed by John, his face close to hers as he clasped her against his chest.

"You're being stubborn, Rachel Crewes. I told you we were both sleeping on the air mattress."

"Put me down, John," she whispered urgently. Her voice was the only weapon she had, since her arms were inside the sleeping bag.

"I intend to. On the air mattress."

"John, we can't sleep together. It would be too—" She didn't know exactly how to explain what it would be unless she used the word *torturous*. And she didn't want to give away that much about her feelings.

"I'm not going to make love to you until you're willing, Rachel. I promise you that. Tonight, we'll just sleep. But it will be together, on the air mattress, not you huddled up on the rocks and me over here. That's dumb."

Before she could organize any logical reply, he placed her on the soft cushion and started unzipping the sleeping bag.

"Scoot over unless you want me to lie down on top of you."

She scurried to the other side, pulling her pillow with her. His suggestive remark hadn't helped matters.

He plopped his pillow down beside her, slid into the sleeping bag and turned off the flashlight. The immediate response of her body to the comfort of the mattress almost overcame her response to John's body next to hers. She pressed against the zipper on the far side, trying to allow as much space between them as possible, but his heat stole beneath the cover to envelop her.

Just the thought of his long legs next to hers, his broad chest only a heartbeat away, made her breathing speed up. *I'm going to be panting like a dog if I'm not careful.* She concentrated on taking deep breaths, hoping to keep her mind off his nearness.

"Relax, Rachel. We're just going to sleep," he repeated.

Yeah, right. Did he really believe it would be that easy? To distract herself, she thought of several names she'd like to call John Crewes for that calm remark. When a slight snore interrupted her thoughts several minutes later, she turned to stare at him in the darkness.

He was asleep? While she was lying here feeling tortured, he had drifted off to sleep? She fought the urge to slam her elbow into his chest. She hated suffering alone. Especially when the suffering was his fault.

If he hadn't kissed her under the stars, if he weren't so sexy, so loving, she'd be able to resist him.

She shifted in the sleeping bag, and her arm brushed against his chest. Softly moaning, she moved away. Then one foot encountered a strong leg. She ran her toes against the hair on his leg, unable to resist the little tease.

Abruptly, he shifted, looping one leg over hers.

Holding her breath, she waited to see if he'd awaken, but he didn't. She released the tension with a sigh. Relaxing against him felt heavenly. Could she trust him?

He was asleep and seemed to be a deep sleeper. And he'd proved she could trust him when she was awake.

Maybe she should follow John's example and just go to sleep. And dream of running her hands all over his big, strong body, of having him wrap his arms around her, of loving her.

It was so tempting to give in to the desire that filled her. But in a year it would all be over. And her heart would be broken.

No, she couldn't give in. But she could dream…just a little.

A LOUD NOISE BROUGHT Rachel partially awake.

"What's that?" she mumbled.

"Just thunder. I think it's raining," John's voice sounded beside her. "Nothing to worry about. Go back to sleep."

Feeling secure, Rachel obeyed him automatically, her eyes drifting shut. His hand rubbed her stomach, beneath her T-shirt, and she stirred again, sighing with pleasure.

"I'll bet you were beautiful when you were pregnant with Jacey," he muttered.

She half laughed, half moaned as he continued stroking her. His thigh moved atop her leg, an easy feat since they were pressed, spoon-fashion, together. It felt so natural, as if they'd always slept like that, that she only settled against him more. Dimly feeling his arousal, she felt as if she were suspended, waiting for him to bring her fully awake. When he only held her, his hand resting against her stomach, she drifted back to sleep.

"MOMMY SAID WE shouldn't wake them up," Lisbeth whispered to Jacey. When Jacey didn't respond, she tugged on her shirt. "Jacey!" she whispered louder.

Jacey turned around, irritated with her friend. "I'm not going to wake them up," she whispered in return.

"I'm just going to get my bucket and shovel. Mommy let me bring them so I could play in the sand."

Jacey returned to her task of slowly unzipping the tent flap. That wasn't her only purpose, of course, but she couldn't tell Lisbeth that she wanted to see if her plan had worked. She wanted to see if her mommy and daddy were sleeping in the same bed the way Lisbeth's had.

The first thing she'd done when she'd awakened this morning was to look at Lisbeth's parents. Just as Lisbeth had said, they were in the big sleeping bag together. Lisbeth's daddy had his arm over her mommy.

Lisbeth had told her last night, before her parents came to bed, that sometimes she got jealous of her mommy because she got more attention from her new daddy than Lisbeth did. Jacey had thought about it, but she didn't feel that way.

She knew John loved her. She couldn't explain it, but she knew. Just as she knew her mommy loved her.

She also knew mommies and daddies had to love each other if they were to stay married. That's why she had to help her mommy and John love each other. And it seemed to her the best way to do that was for them to do things like Lisbeth's parents.

Her heart beating faster, Jacey lifted the tent flap and fearfully searched the shadowy darkness. Had her plan worked?

Looking at Lisbeth over her shoulder, she motioned for her friend to stay back. Then she tiptoed into the tent, letting the flap fall behind her.

She snuck up to the edge of the air mattress and stared down at Mommy and John. They were even better than Lisbeth's parents, she decided, because they were both snuggling together. Lots closer, too.

In fact, she wondered if maybe Lisbeth had been wrong. 'Cause the way they were sleeping, there was lots of room left over for Jacey. That would be neat, the three of them in bed together. She couldn't hold back a giggle at the thought.

"Jacey?" John whispered, raising his head to look at her.

"Sorry. I came to get my bucket and shovel."

"Okay, sweetheart. I think they're still in the back of the station wagon. It's not locked. Be quiet and don't wake your mommy."

"I won't. Bye-bye."

Jacey emerged from the tent with all the excitement of Christmas morning. It had worked! They were sleeping together, just like a real family.

JOHN LAID HIS HEAD BACK down on the pillow, giving himself a minute to evaluate the situation. He was in the sleeping bag with Rachel, his body plastered to hers, his hands in inappropriate places, and all he wanted to do was wake her up slowly and make unending love to her.

Not exactly what he'd promised.

If Rachel awoke before he extricated himself, she'd never forgive him. Or trust him again.

With a reluctance that was almost overpowering, John slid out of the sleeping bag. Once he was standing, he took off the jogging shorts he'd worn to bed and slipped into jeans and a polo shirt.

Rachel hadn't moved at all. After picking up his tennis shoes and socks, he peered over the bed until he could see her face. She was breathing evenly, her eyes closed, and he remembered with longing the rhythm of her breathing matching his through the night.

With a sigh, he tiptoed from the tent.

RACHEL WAITED A FULL five minutes after John's departure before she moved. She didn't want him to know Jacey had awakened her when she had John. Or that Rachel had realized how closely entwined their bodies had been. Or how heavenly it had felt.

After all her protests of the night before, John must think her a terrible tease. She hadn't stuck to her side of the sleeping bag even before she'd fallen asleep. With guilty pleasure, she remembered touching him, relaxing against him. Then there was a vague memory of a thunderstorm and John comforting her. His comfort had been so stimulating, it was a wonder she hadn't begged him to make love to her.

What was she going to do? Every time the man got near her, her heart raced, her hands itched to touch him. She longed for his kisses.

How was she going to continue to resist her husband?

Chapter Fifteen

First thing Monday morning, John made arrangements to buy Rachel's house in her name. The landlord had been a little reluctant to sell, but John had gone above market value to entice him. Since John wasn't financing his purchase, they agreed to close on it Thursday.

Rachel was going to be angry. But John didn't care. He was enjoying buying things for her. Quite a change from his first marriage.

At least, finding ways to give gifts to Rachel took his mind off sleeping with her. And after Saturday night, that hadn't been an easy task. When he'd crawled into bed last night, he'd missed her warmth next to him. He'd missed more than her warmth. He wanted to make love to her. For the rest of his life.

He spun around in his chair and stared out the office window. "Okay, I admit it," he professed to an invisible audience. "I love her."

He'd promised himself he'd never fall in love again. But he had. And he didn't regret it.

At least this time was different. He'd fallen in love with Jacey first. When he'd seen Rachel, he'd wanted her, but he hadn't loved her. But Rachel's courage, determination and big heart had him falling faster than a bungee jumper.

As for Jacey, she was one child in a million. He'd never realized he wanted children, a family, until the little moppet had looked over his fence.

And even though he bought the house next door for Rachel, he didn't intend for her to move back into it. He wanted her to move, all right, but only across the hall into his bed. Permanently.

"Mr. Wester is on line one," his secretary said through the intercom.

"Thanks. Hi, David," he said cheerfully as he picked up the phone. Today he was ready to take on the world.

"John, I hope I didn't interrupt anything important."

"Nope. Well, I was just thinking about how much I love my wife and daughter, but nothing other than that."

"Glad to hear it. The three of you made a welcome addition to the weekend. And that's what I called about."

"Yes?" John said cautiously.

"I want you, Rachel and Jacey to be on the video I'm going to produce about blended families. What do you say?"

"Don't you use actors for those?" John asked, stalling for time. He didn't think Rachel would agree to David's request.

"Never!" David exclaimed, sounding offended. "We always interview real people. We're not using smoke and mirrors, John. We only tell the truth."

"I appreciate that, David. But I'm not sure Rachel would agree to your request. She's a very private person, you know." So private she didn't even want to talk to John, much less the viewers of the video.

"I can understand that, John, but the three of you would be really terrific. Would you ask her and see what she says?"

"Well, of course, David, I'll ask her. Can I give you her answer tomorrow? She teaches, you know, and it's almost impossible to talk to her during the day."

"Sure. You can have several days to make up your minds. We're doing a bare-bones script, though most of it is impromptu. We won't be ready to make any hard decisions until the end of the week."

"Thanks. I'll let you know."

He hung up the phone and thought about his promise. He was pretty sure Rachel would say no, but at least he had something to talk to her about. All of Sunday, Rachel had avoided even discussing the weather with him. As soon as Jacey had been tucked in last night, she'd retreated to her bedroom, claiming papers to grade.

With David's request, he'd at least have her attention for a few minutes. Maybe they could reestablish the friendship that had been growing between them. He had to have that as a beginning.

Because he was determined that one day, when she was ready, Rachel would be his wife in every sense of the word. But first he had to prove to her that she could trust him. Her experience with Jacey's father had left her unable to trust. Especially sexual attraction.

With a groan, he promised himself he'd keep his distance, not touch her, unless she asked him to. He laughed. Yeah, right. That was hardly likely to happen.

He turned back to his work. Time to get busy if he wanted to get out of the office at a decent hour. And dinner with Jacey and Rachel was on the top of his list.

AFTER THE CAMPING TRIP and the success she'd had bringing her mommy and John together, Jacey was happy on Monday morning. She couldn't wait to talk to Lisbeth about the fun they'd had together over the weekend.

"Hi, Lisbeth!" she called out, racing across the room to her best friend.

"Hi." Lisbeth didn't smile or move. She remained slumped across the top of her desk.

"Are you sick?"

"No."

Jacey leaned over to peer into Lisbeth's face. "Then what's wrong?"

"Nothing."

"I mean really, Lisbeth. Did you get in trouble?"

"No."

Jacey rounded the desk and put her arm around her friend. "I had fun this weekend."

"Me, too."

"Then why are you so sad?"

"I can't tell you."

"Why not?"

"Mommy said."

A sudden thought struck Jacey and she turned fearful eyes on her friend. "You're not going to move away, are you?"

"No! It's not that bad."

"Then—"

"At your desks, children. It's time to start class," Mrs. Wilson called out.

"Later," Jacey promised as she moved to take her place.

When recess was announced after reading circles, Jacey returned to her friend's side. "Are you still sad?"

"Yes."

"I won't tell anyone if you tell me what made you sad."

Lisbeth looked around and then turned back to Jacey. "You promise not to tell anyone?"

"I promise."

"Mommy may have another baby."

"Wow!" Jacey exclaimed, her eyes widening in surprise. "That's neat."

"No, it's not. They'll love the new baby and not me. It will be Daddy's real baby."

"Can't they still love you?" Jacey asked, frowning.

Lisbeth shook her head, her bottom lip pushed out. "I don't think so."

"Lots of families have more than one kid."

"Yeah, but they all have the same daddy. Daddy's not really mine." Lisbeth propped her head up and sighed.

"How do mommies have babies?" Jacey asked, as she pondered what Lisbeth had said. Would her mommy have a baby? Would John not love Jacey if Mommy did have a baby?

"I don't know. I guess it's when they get married. It just happens."

Jacey stared across the room, her finger in her mouth, as she thought about what Lisbeth had revealed.

"JACEY, THAT BAG IS too heavy for you, sweetie. You take this one, and I'll carry the big ones." Rachel set a small bag on the tailgate of the station wagon for Jacey. She liked to help her mother, and Rachel encouraged her. She believed Jacey should share in the chores even as young as she was.

"Okay, Mommy."

They reached the door and Rachel balanced a bag on her knee as she leaned against the wall to fish out the key. When she got the door open, Jacey preceded her into the house.

"In the kitchen, sweetie. Just put your bag on the breakfast table." Rachel did the same before going back to the car for another load. "If you'll get my book bag from the back seat, that would be a big help."

"Okay."

Rachel frowned as she watched her daughter go out the door ahead of her. Jacey had been remarkably silent today. Something must be bothering her.

"Jacey?"

Her daughter turned around as she reached the car door. "Yes, Mommy?"

"Is anything wrong?" She watched as Jacey immediately turned away from her.

"No."

Concern filled Rachel. She'd always taught her daughter to be truthful. Lately that rule had gone by the wayside, but she was surprised that Jacey wouldn't tell her what was bothering her. And something obviously was. Rachel postponed her motherly inquisition until they'd finished unloading the groceries. Once they were back in the kitchen, she and Jacey began putting away their purchases.

"Put the cookies and crackers on the third shelf, okay?" Rachel had reorganized John's pantry as soon as she'd moved in. And filled it. A few canned goods and a box of crackers had been all she'd found.

As she gathered up the fresh fruit and vegetables, she said, as offhandedly as possible, "You know, when something is wrong, it helps to talk about it."

Jacey shot her a look out of the corner of her eye before she concentrated on stacking the boxes she carried on the third shelf. "I know," she finally said in a low voice.

"Then why won't you talk to me?" Rachel asked softly.

Jacey trudged back to the grocery sacks as if all the weight of the world was on her shoulders. "Okay. I need to know how you make babies."

Rachel blinked several times, hoping her shock wasn't showing on her face. Without answering, she walked to the refrigerator and opened it to deposit the fruit and vegetables. Then she faced her daughter.

"Why do you want to know?"

"Someone at school today was talking about getting a baby. I just wondered."

"I see. Well, a baby grows in the mommy's stomach until it's big enough to hold, and a doctor takes it out at the hospital."

"How does it get in there in the first place? Do you have one in your stomach?"

"No! No, I don't, sweetie. And babies—babies happen when a mommy and daddy make love... sometimes."

"Oh."

Rachel braced herself for another question, because she could see in Jacey's face that she wasn't satisfied. The sound of the front door opening interrupted them, however.

"Daddy's home!" Jacey exclaimed and ran for the front of the house.

Rachel returned to the task of putting away groceries, trying to organize her thoughts as she worked. She suspected Jacey would ask more questions. Rachel only hoped she saved them for bedtime and didn't ask them in front of John.

John and Jacey entered the kitchen together, her arms around his neck as he carried her.

"Grocery shopping? I didn't realize—I haven't given you any money for groceries, Rachel," John said as he looked at the sacks on the table.

"I had some money."

"But that wasn't our deal."

No, it wasn't. But she didn't like remembering their deal. It made his actions seem cold-blooded, based on money. Idiot! When was she going to wake up? Of course, that was the reason for his behavior.

"I'll open you a checking account tomorrow. And I need to get you some credit cards, too," he said with a frown, as if making a mental list.

"Really, John, it's not necessary."

"Yes, it is."

She couldn't bear another argument. They brought her too close to the edge. She did much better if she stayed in control. "Dinner isn't ready yet. It will be in about half an hour."

"No hurry. Want me and Jacey to put things away while you get started? That way we can keep each other company."

Jacey seemed delighted with the idea and wriggled out of his arms to the floor. "Yeah. Come on. I'll show you how Mommy likes everything."

"Good idea, little one. I could use a few lessons." He sent Rachel that sideways grin of his and she turned her back on the two of them.

Rachel found it unnerving to work with John in the same room. Fortunately her dinner plans were simple. After they stowed away the groceries, John and Jacey settled down at the table to chat with her while she worked.

Jacey finished telling John about Earl's latest escapade at school. Before he could comment, she asked another question.

"John, do you and Mommy make love?"

"Jacey!" Rachel exclaimed, her face bright red.

Jacey frowned at her mother. "What, Mommy? You said that's how babies are made and I just wondered—"

John didn't appear nearly as disturbed as she was, Rachel noted.

"What your mommy means, sweetheart, is that people don't talk about making love. It's very personal, just between two people."

"Like you and Mommy?"

"Like me and Mommy."

"Then how will I know?"

"Know what?"

John's question was perfectly natural, but Rachel knew the answer and wasn't anxious for Jacey to explain.

"Jacey, I don't think—"

"If we're going to have a baby," the child replied, ignoring her mother's protest.

"Ah," John said, as if he understood how little girls thought. "Someone at school must be going to have a baby—I mean, their mommy."

"Maybe," Jacey said.

"I knew school was educational," John said to Rachel, a grin on his face. "But I thought it was from books."

Rachel couldn't hold back a smile in return. "It's called sharing."

"Yeah. Well, little one, if we have a baby, we'll be sure to let you know way in advance."

"But why would you want a baby? You have me." Jacey's little face was anxious as she looked up at John.

Rachel suddenly realized the reason for Jacey's questions. Before she could reassure her, however, John spoke.

"A baby would never replace you, Jacey. We could have a hundred babies, and none of them would be you." He cuddled her closer to him. "Have you ever had a favorite baby doll?"

She nodded, one finger in her mouth.

"Well, what if you got a big stuffed lion that you really loved?"

"I did, John. You got it for me."

"I know, sweetheart. Did that big lion make you love your baby doll any less?"

She shook her head no. He hadn't resolved all her questions, however. "But the baby would be your baby and I'm not."

Rachel moved over to the table and sat down in the chair next to John. They had reached the crux of the problem, she knew. Surprisingly, she trusted John to give the right answer.

"That's not true, Jacey. You see, you and I chose each other. You picked me to be your daddy, and I picked you to be my little girl. If we have a baby, we have to take it no matter what it looks like. It could be as ugly as sin!"

"John!" Rachel protested, but she couldn't subdue her grin.

John grinned back at her, but he talked to Jacey. "It could even be a boy!" he exclaimed in mock horror.

Jacey giggled. "Like Earl!"

"Oh, no! Not like Earl!" he said, hamming it up just like Jacey.

He tickled her tummy and they both laughed. Rachel sighed. She'd known John would make Jacey feel good. Whatever else she thought about him, she knew he loved Jacey and would never hurt her.

Jacey put her arms back around his neck. "I love you, John. I'm glad you chose me."

"I'm glad you chose me, too," he assured her, hugging her to him. Over Jacey's shoulder, he stared at Rachel.

"We mustn't forget Mommy," Jacey said, pulling away from John and scrambling out of his lap to come to her mother. "I love you, too, Mommy."

"Me, too, Mommy," John said, with that teasing glint in his eyes.

Rachel smiled back at him, grateful for the tender care he gave Jacey. And her heart ached with a yearning she tried to resist. But she couldn't. She wanted him to say those words and mean them.

With Jacey still in her arms, John pulled her to her feet and embraced both of them, his lips covering Rachel's in a sweet kiss.

"Help! You're squeezing me," Jacey protested with a giggle.

John pulled back and took Jacey from Rachel's arms. "Okay, okay, we'd better let your mommy cook dinner. I'm starving!"

"Me, too!" Jacey said, curling up in his lap as he sat down.

Rachel turned away from them, hoping they wouldn't notice her trembling. John's tenderness unnerved her.

"You know, I've been thinking," Jacey said after a minute.

"What have you been thinking?" John asked in an absentminded tone.

"I think we *should* have a baby."

Chapter Sixteen

John rapped on Rachel's door. Just like last night, as soon as Jacey had been put to bed, Rachel had retreated to her bedroom to grade papers.

He'd suggested she use the dining room table, or make herself comfortable in the den. She refused both options. He was pretty sure he was the stumbling block, not his house.

The door opened only a couple of inches. Rachel peered through the narrow opening. "Yes?"

"I need to talk to you."

Her eyes widened in alarm. "I'm sorry about Jacey's questions, John. I'll explain to her that—"

"I'm not concerned with Jacey's questions," he told her hurriedly. "I'm glad she feels free to ask them."

Rachel didn't appear to be greatly reassured, but she didn't close the door on him, either.

"May I come in?" he asked. He read the reluctance in her face, but she finally opened the door wider.

"Yes, of course."

He walked in, noting the neatness of the room except for several stacks of paper spread out on the bed. "How's the grading going?"

"Slowly."

She continued to watch him with big eyes. He knew he had to explain his request before she would relax—if she would, even then. "David called today."

"Is something wrong?" she asked anxiously, taking a step closer to him.

In response, he put his hands on her shoulders, rubbing back and forth in an attempt to comfort her. "No, of course not. He said we were terrific on the camping trip." His attempt to reassure her was having an adverse effect on his concentration. Somehow his gaze remained fastened on her full lips, and he fought the urge to kiss her.

"Then why did he call?"

"Because he's going ahead with the new video series—you know, about blended families. And—and he wants us to be in it."

She drew back, horror on her face. "No! John, we couldn't!"

"Well, we could, but I agree it probably wouldn't be a good idea," he admitted, easing her back close to him. "But David thinks we'd be a terrific addition. And I promised I'd ask you."

"The answer is no." Her response was emphatic, with no room for discussion.

"Just so I can explain it to David, why?"

"Why? John, it's bad enough that we're lying to David and his wife and all the other people we've met. But to make a video for nationwide distribution? That would be horrible."

Privately, he agreed with her. But he didn't want to bring their talk to an end. "Is it that hard to pretend to love me?" He kept his question light and added a grin to let her know he wasn't serious.

"You're just looking for compliments, Mr. Crewes," she said and pushed at his chest playfully.

He captured her hand against him, loving the warm tingling her touch brought. "Everyone needs a little encouragement."

"Not you!"

"Yes, me. Surely you can tell me *something* you like about me." When she gave him a stubborn look, he added, "I can name several things I like about you. The way you care for Jacey. And your cooking. I'm going to have to watch my weight or I'll be a blimp by the end of the year."

He looked at her expectantly.

"Okay, okay, you're wonderful with Jacey. No father could be more loving or patient." She stopped but he raised an eyebrow to encourage her. "And—and you're wonderfully generous."

"Thank you. My turn, again." He eased her body against his, fully in his embrace, as he said, "You have beautiful blue eyes, and the softest, sexiest lips I've ever seen."

Her cheeks flushed with color and she tried to pull away. "John, this is getting out of hand."

"You're just trying to stop because you don't like anything about me," he teased, a mock pout on his face.

"No, I— Okay, you have the most expressive eyebrows I've ever seen."

"That's not very sexy," he complained.

She responded to his challenge, her eyes twinkling and her lips smiling. "You would prefer me to tell you that you have magnificent buns?"

"Really? Well, they can't compare to yours." He let his hands slip to that part of her anatomy.

"John! Behave yourself. We're just having a discussion."

"Yeah. An adult version of show-and-tell. And I'd like you to model that piece of underwear you were dangling under my nose the other night. I've had a lot of dreams about you in that black bra."

Her cheeks grew even redder and she unconsciously looked down at her bosom.

He groaned. "You're wearing it now, aren't you?" He had his answer in the guilty, self-conscious look on her face, but she attempted to deny it.

"Of course not! Don't be ridiculous!" She tried to push away from him, but the movement only stimulated his already overheated body.

His arms tightened around her and his lips captured hers as he gave in to the volcanic urges he'd been resisting. The moment he'd realized she was wearing the black bra beneath the sedate print blouse that topped her jeans, he was lost.

If she made any effort to resist him, he didn't notice it. Her arms encircled his neck and she ran her fingers through his hair. He took advantage of her surrender to press her against him from their knees to their shoulders. Her breasts seemed to burrow into his chest as he kissed her, and he brought one hand up to stroke them.

She gasped as his mouth trailed kisses from her throbbing lips to her neck before returning to her lips.

This time, when he urged her to open to him, she didn't hesitate. Their tongues dueled, both winning, as his hands caressed every inch of her. When his fingers settled on the buttons of her blouse, she was too busy kissing him back to notice.

The unbuttoning was a slow process because he grew distracted several times. Rachel slid her hands beneath his knit shirt and caressed his body. He wanted to strip them both naked immediately, but he was too busy tasting the nectar of her lips. He couldn't bear the thought of breaking off the kiss.

Eventually, however, he pulled apart her blouse to reveal the black lace bra in all its glory, her aroused nipples pushing against the delicate lace, begging to escape.

He trailed his lips along the edges of the bra, his tongue dipping into the valley between her breasts. Rachel's panting as she pressed against him, her lips covering his forehead and then moving to his ear, only inspired him to greater liberties. The bra fastened in front and he freed her swollen breasts from their enclosure before covering them with his mouth.

Rachel whimpered and one leg curled around his hips as she sought to be even closer to him. More than willing to grant her wish, he lifted her, his hands encasing her hips, and moved to the bed. Even as her head touched its softness, he was on top of her, his mouth saluting each breast before moving back to the softness of her lips.

Lost in the storm of passion they'd created, he was totally unprepared for Rachel's reaction. Wrenching her lips from his, she began shoving him off her frantically.

"The papers! The papers!" she screamed.

Her urgency slowly penetrated the fog of physical reaction. "What's wrong?" he gasped.

"We're crinkling the papers! My students' papers!" Rachel shoved harder and John slid to his knees beside the bed. Rachel pushed herself up, her concentration on her schoolwork, unconscious of her gaping blouse and full breasts. John, however, couldn't take his eyes from the view. Such enticement led him to touch again, but this time Rachel wasn't receptive.

She slapped at his hands and pulled her blouse together with one hand. "Stop it, John. We have to stop it."

He did stop, but as he stood, he asked her, "Why?"

"Because we're ruining my papers."

"I have a big bed without any papers. Come on." He took her hand and pulled her from the bed.

"No! No, I'm not going to your bed. We're making a mistake, John. This is a temporary marriage, remember? We promised not to—to do this sort of thing."

"I don't remember promising that," he said, his brows lowered.

She pressed her swollen lips together, and John could hardly restrain himself. The memory of their softness crushed against his mouth, their generosity, their caresses against his skin, almost unleashed what little control he had.

"*I* promised. No more, John, please."

He recognized the determination in her voice. But he regretted it. "Whatever you say," he muttered and turned away. He looked behind him once as he closed the door, but she had her back to him.

When he reached his room, he fell on the bed with a groan. He'd seen her in the black lace bra, as he'd wanted. Now the only question he had was, How would he ever sleep again? Visions of Rachel without any bra at all were sure to remain in his head for the rest of his days. As well as the taste and touch of her. He would be miserable without her.

As she heard the door close, Rachel sank back down on the cleared area of the bed. The riot in which her senses were participating was a protest against John's withdrawal. They begged for completion, but she'd refused.

She bit her bottom lip until tears appeared in her eyes and then fell, sliding down her cheeks. What was she to do now? How was she to live in such close quarters with the one man in the world she couldn't resist? Shivers raced up and down her spine as she remembered his touch, his kisses, his desire.

Removing the stack of papers from the bed, she slowly undressed. There was no point in trying to work now. She'd never be able to concentrate on the effect of inflation on the value of the dollar. Or on one student's estimation of the president's policy on individual rights.

Her body was clamoring for its right to be loved. By one sexy, nearby male. That was all she could think about. She slipped on her nightgown and turned off the light. Sliding into her lonely bed, she lay there, aching, wanting. How much self-denial could one person bear?

RACHEL MADE SURE SHE was occupied with the toaster when she heard John's steps on the stairs.

"Mommy, John's here," Jacey sang out.

Reaching for a coffee mug, Rachel filled it and took it to the table, but her gaze never reached his face. "The toast will be ready in a moment."

"Thanks," John said, but still Rachel didn't look at him.

"What's wrong, John? Are you thinking about something again?" Jacey asked. "Like when we visited Lisbeth?"

Out of the corner of her eye, Rachel saw John reach out and rub Jacey's head.

"Yeah, baby, I'm thinking. Have a good day at school," he said and stood.

"But you haven't eaten your breakfast," Rachel protested, looking at him for the first time. She was shocked to see circles under his eyes, a weary look on his face.

"I'm not hungry." He tried to smile, but all he managed was a grimace.

With a muttered goodbye, he left the house.

Rachel automatically buttered the toast that popped up and then filled her mug a second time and sat down at the table beside her daughter.

"Do you think John has a sick tummy?" Jacey asked, concern in her voice.

"What? Sick? Um, no, sweetie, I don't think he's sick. Maybe he worked too late last night." Or, maybe, like her, he hadn't been able to go to sleep until the wee hours of the morning.

After dropping Jacey off at kindergarten, Rachel continued on to her school, but she ran on automatic pilot. What was the matter with her? She'd had other nights when she couldn't sleep.

But it wasn't only the lack of sleep that bothered Rachel. It was her situation. She had agreed to live with a man, her husband, for an entire year. But she'd insisted that it be a marriage in name only. Her logic was faultless. The parting at the end of that year would be much easier without any physical complications.

But the year would be misery.

As last night had been.

All day long she debated her choices. It was during second period that she admitted to herself that she loved John Crewes. A student had stood waiting for an answer to his questions for several minutes, finally prodding her.

She apologized, but she was operating in a fog. Her mind was taken up with John. Loving him didn't make her choices any easier. Fifth period, when a student came in late and she ignored him, one of her favorite pupils raised his hand.

"Are you all right, Ms. Cason?"

"What?"

"Are you all right? Chuck came in late for the second time this week and you just smiled at him."

She sighed and turned to Chuck, who was now glaring at the other boy. "No, I'm not feeling well, so I guess you got lucky, Chuck. Don't try it again."

"No, Ms. Cason. I won't. Uh, Ms. Cason?"

"Yes?"

"We all noticed that ring on your finger. Did you get married?"

Rachel stared at the gold band. All the other days before coming to school she'd carefully secreted the ring in her purse. Today, as distracted as she was, she'd forgotten.

She looked at all the interested faces in her classroom. Finally, she admitted, "Yes, I got married."

A spontaneous cheer arose and she stared at them in surprise. "I didn't know it would please you so much," she said, but she also hadn't known how much it would please *her* to admit her marriage.

"We just think it's neat," Julieann, a cheerleader with a penchant for the romantic, said with a sigh.

"Well, we need to continue with our discussion about the Korean War," Rachel insisted, determination in her voice. As if admitting her marriage to her students had been the answer she was seeking, she sloughed off all the self-questions and got down to work.

Rachel left school as soon as her last class ended. She didn't pack up any more papers to grade. She didn't straighten the odds and ends on her desk as she usually did. Her thoughts were on something, someone else. She had an errand to run before she picked up Jacey. A very private errand.

Once that had been accomplished, she picked up her daughter and then stopped at the grocery store. She was going to fix a special dinner this evening.

"We're going to have strawberry shortcake?" Jacey asked in surprise.

"Yes, we are."

"But it's not my birthday."

"I know, sweetie, but—but I feel like celebrating."

"Why?"

Rachel smiled as she pulled into the driveway. John's driveway. "Because we're happy."

"Yeah!" Jacey agreed, a big grin on her face.

"Come on. We've got a lot to do before John gets home."

Jacey, always willing to do something John might like, hurried to her mother's assistance.

Two hours later, the strawberry shortcake was stored in the refrigerator, the steaks were ready to go on the grill on the patio, where the baked potatoes were already roasting, a freshly made salad awaited its dressing, and hot rolls were just coming out of the oven.

Rachel kept looking at her watch.

"Where's John?" Jacey asked for the thousandth time.

"I don't know."

The ringing of the phone was her answer, and she approached it with dread.

"Rachel, it's John. I'm going to run late this evening. I hope that isn't a problem."

Rachel looked at all their preparations. "No, not at all. I have dinner ready, but I can reheat it when you get here."

"Don't worry about me. I'll probably grab something here. I'm not sure when I'll be in."

Apparently John had made some decisions today, also, and his didn't resemble hers. But she wouldn't go down without a fight.

"Jacey and I made a special dinner. I think you'll like it." She hated to use her child but she did. "Jacey will be very disappointed if you don't eat some of it."

There was a long pause, and she held her breath for his answer. "Are you sure you want me to come home now?"

"Yes, I'm sure."

"I'll be there in twenty minutes."

There was a click as he hung up, but it was Jacey tugging on her sleeve that reminded her to hang up.

"What did he say, Mommy?"

"He's on his way home, sweetie. He didn't want to disappoint you."

Jacey gave her a satisfied smile and said, "He's the best."

"Yes, he certainly is."

True to his word, John pulled into the drive almost to the minute he'd promised. Jacey greeted him at the door and led him to the table. He gave Rachel a weary smile, reminding her of herself before she got her second wind.

He looked better after eating the meal they'd prepared.

"Rachel, that was a terrific dinner. But I hate for you to go to so much trouble after teaching all day." His gaze roamed her body as he spoke, and she felt herself heating up.

"I enjoyed it. And Jacey helped me a lot."

"Just what did you do to help Mommy?" John asked, reaching for Jacey and taking her into his lap.

I washed the potatoes and wrapped them in that shiny stuff," Jacey replied importantly. "And I helped Mommy wash the strawberries."

"Strawberries? I didn't eat any strawberries," John said. Jacey responded with a giggle she tried to hide beneath her hand.

"We made our special dessert, only served on special occasions," Rachel explained.

John groaned and rubbed his stomach, his flat stomach, and Rachel's mouth went dry. "I don't know if I have room for a special dessert."

"It's got whipped cream, too," Jacey added, her eyes glowing in anticipation.

"Well, maybe just a little piece," John said. "And if I can't finish mine, I'm sure you'll help me, right, Jacey?"

Jacey didn't need to help John. They both cleaned their plates. Only Rachel didn't finish her dessert. Her gaze remained fixed on the man across from her, as did her thoughts.

Had she made the right decision? Yes. They couldn't go on as they had. It was too hard on both of them. Her gaze traced his lips, his shoulders, his chest, and strawberry shortcake held little interest for her. She had a better dessert planned for later. Much later.

John entertained Jacey while Rachel cleaned the kitchen, although he offered to help. Rachel refused. She didn't need him near her now. There was no point in suffering needlessly.

She mopped the kitchen floor after the dishes were done. Anything to keep her mind off what was to come. Even with the extra work, she still had time left before Jacey's bedtime. When she suggested a swim, Jacey didn't hesitate.

"Wow! This really is a special night, Mommy. I really can swim in the pool?" she asked, looking at John.

"Sure, if your mommy wants to. Do you have a swimsuit?"

Jacey nodded even as she hit the floor, running.

"You can't go into the pool until I get my suit on," Rachel reminded her as she disappeared.

"I'll go change, too," John said, standing.

"You don't have to. I thought you might like a little time to yourself. Jacey's kept you pretty busy tonight."

Their gazes met and Rachel almost fell into his arms at the longing she saw there.

"No, it's better if I swim. I didn't sleep too well last night."

Although her cheeks reddened, Rachel just nodded and went upstairs to change. The new swimsuit revealed a lot more of her than her old one, but she wasn't worried about that tonight. It seemed to be a consideration for John, however, as he first caught sight of her.

He swallowed several times before saying, "Nice suit, Rachel."

"Ready?" Jacey pleaded, dancing from one foot to the other.

"Yes, we're ready," she assured her child, but her gaze remained on John. Only the splash as Jacey entered the pool distracted her attention.

An hour later, she tucked an exhausted-but-contented Jacey into her bed.

"Mommy, this was the best night. Isn't it great living with John?"

"Just great, sweetie." After her prayers and a goodnight kiss, Jacey was asleep almost before Rachel could leave her room.

Half an hour later, after careful preparation, Rachel crossed the hall and knocked on John's door.

"Come in," he called.

As he'd been last week when she'd stormed into his room, John was propped up in his bed, reading a newspaper. His gaze widened as she walked into his room and closed the door behind her.

"Is something wrong?" he asked, sitting up.

"No. But I bought something for you today." She held out a brown paper bag. "I thought you might want to—to use it this evening."

Chapter Seventeen

John stared at Rachel as she stood beside his bed. He'd spent very little time sleeping last night after their aborted lovemaking. Now she was standing there, wearing a sexy ice-blue negligee, her hair falling about her shoulders, smiling at him, holding out a paper sack.

What was she trying to do—kill him? Did she think showing him what he was missing would help him sleep? The woman was crazy.

"Look, thanks, Rachel, but you didn't need to buy me anything. I'm about ready for bed, so why don't we, uh, talk in the morning." He snapped the newspaper and forced his gaze from her sexy presence to the printed word.

"But, John, I made a special trip. Won't you at least look at what I bought you?"

"Rachel, I'm really not in the mood for games. I didn't get much sleep last night, and the swim almost did me in. You're not helping the situation by coming in here dressed like that. I think it's highly unfair of you to do so."

She looked down at the gown she was wearing and then back at him. "It kind of goes with my gift."

"Unless you've got an aphrodisiac in that bag, I think you're mistaken," he growled, his patience fading fast. Was she a tease?

Her full lips formed a pout that almost drove him crazy. "You think you'll need an aphrodisiac?"

As he was about to snap an answer, he came to an abrupt halt. The look in her eyes finally told him he was missing something.

"No," he replied, drawing out his answer, "I wouldn't need an aphrodisiac to want to make love to you, Rachel." He watched her every move, wondering what she was up to. There was a surging hope in him that she might want to take up where they'd left off last night, but she was going to have to make that clear to him. He couldn't stand that much frustration again.

"Good. Take your present, John."

With his gaze never leaving her, he reached over for the sack. "What is it?"

She crossed her arms under her breasts, only drawing his attention to their ripe fullness, and said nothing. For the first time, he noted some signs of nervousness.

"Are you going to answer me?"

"I hope all the answer you need is in the sack. I certainly went to enough trouble and embarrassment to buy it."

Although he was reluctant to look away from her, he unfolded the top of the bag and looked inside. His eyebrows snapped together and he upended the sack, dropping three boxes on the bed.

"I—I didn't know what kind, so I picked three. I hope they're—"

"Rachel!"

"I didn't think we should take any chances. I mean, I know it's only for a year but—"

"Rachel!"

"I don't think we'd survive a year like last night," she finished with a rush.

"I know I wouldn't," he assured her fervently, swinging back the covers and reaching for her at the same time. One of the boxes of condoms fell to the floor, but John ignored it. There were still two more to choose from.

"You're sure?" he asked, already aroused as he pressed her silkily-clad body against him.

"Oh, yes." She sighed as her mouth met his.

John decided he'd been a gentleman and given her a chance to withdraw. Any more discussion could take place later. Much later.

His briefs joined her negligee on the floor and he pulled her down on the bed with him. She met him more than halfway as he resumed their embrace where they'd left it last night.

Finally, he could touch her everywhere, smooth her soft skin with his fingers, kiss her from one end to the other, feel her beneath him. To his delight, Rachel showed no hesitation in touching him in return. Never had he experienced such joy.

When he entered her, making them one, he did so carefully, knowing it had been a long time for her. But Rachel urged him to greater heights as she stroked his back and moaned softly. The sound was like a crooning that pulled him closer.

Rapidly they progressed until John felt Rachel peak just as he could no longer hold back, and they joined in such passion that the world disappeared. Only sensation and love remained.

When their pounding heartbeats eased, he wrapped her in his embrace, afraid to let her go. He'd dreamed of making love to Rachel, but the reality was more than he'd ever imagined. He was afraid that if he turned her loose, he might never hold her again.

"Rachel?"

"Mmm?" she murmured sleepily, her lips moving against his neck.

"You... That was incredible."

Although she said nothing, she pressed even closer to him, her breasts flattening against his chest, stirring him again.

He ran a hand down her back, enjoying touching her soft skin, then placed kisses on her neck.

"I should go back to my room," she whispered.

"No! No, don't go."

"But Jacey—"

"We're married, Rachel. You're my wife, remember? Married couples get to do this all the time." He held his breath, afraid she would refuse to stay.

"I don't see how they have the stamina," she finally said.

"You'll get your second wind," he promised. "After all, you bought three boxes of condoms. You must've had great expectations." He kissed her soft lips before she could answer.

When he raised his head, she reached up to run a finger down the side of his face. "I didn't mean you had to use them all tonight, John. I thought... I mean, we're going to be married a year. I didn't see any point in torturing ourselves as we did last night.''

John frowned. That was the second time she'd mentioned the limit to their marriage. But he had a year—a much better year than he'd expected, after last night. He would convince her to stay. He had to.

"You're right. I'll go buy some more condoms for tomorrow night,'' he told her.

A shiver of pleasure ran through him as she chuckled. "Even you aren't that macho, John Crewes. I doubt we'll need another box for at least two nights.''

"I'll do my best, Mrs. Crewes,'' he assured her, drawing her beneath him again. And he did.

For the second night in a row, Rachel didn't get much sleep. But passion was the reason this time, rather than frustration. When John wakened her at dawn, it took several minutes of his delicious attention before she responded. Afterward, he held her again in his arms, stroking and soothing, making her feel loved and protected.

"You'd better call in sick, sweetheart,'' he murmured. "I haven't let you rest much.''

"You haven't rested, either,'' she returned.

He chuckled—a low sexy laugh that, incredibly, made her want him again. If she didn't control herself, John was going to think she was a nymphomaniac.

"I feel great. Call in sick, and then go back to bed. I'll take care of Jacey.''

"I can't let you do that, John. It wouldn't be fair,'' she mumbled, liking the idea more and more as she thought about it.

"Yes, you can. What's the number to get a substitute?"

Rachel told him and he dialed it, then pressed the receiver to her ear. When the recorder came on, she asked for a substitute teacher to take her classes.

"Now," John whispered, dropping a kiss on her forehead, "go back to sleep. I'll see you this afternoon."

The last she remembered was the sound of the shower in the master bath going on.

WHEN RACHEL FINALLY awoke, it was almost noon. Feeling a shade guilty, she hurried to the shower. The hot, steamy water helped ease the stiffness her night of passion had left. She could scarcely consider their nighttime activities objectively. What little experience she'd had in the past didn't compare with the overpowering desire that filled her when her husband touched her.

She hoped she'd done the right thing. It felt right. It felt incredible, if she was honest. But in the shadowy future, the end of their marriage lingered, mocking her happiness. A year. That was all she had.

Shutting off the water, she wrapped a towel around herself and stepped from the shower. Who knew what could happen in a year? John seemed ... seemed attracted to her. Even as she thought that, she blushed. His attentions the previous night had been more than that, surely.

She harbored hope in her heart that he felt something more than lust for her. He had to. He couldn't make love to her as he had without *some* feeling, could he?

She briskly toweled off, dismissing such disturbing thoughts. Not having had a day to herself in so long, Rachel decided she should avoid such probing questions and make good use of her time. She would move her belongings from the house next door. Then Polly could call her friend.

After several hours of hard work, Rachel made herself a sandwich and sat down at the kitchen table. She was proud of what she'd accomplished. Everything except the furniture was moved in. She'd check with John and see if she should call a mover to handle the larger items.

First, however, she should call her landlord to let him know she was moving out. It wouldn't hurt to tell him about Polly's friend, also. Mr. Lawson had been kind to her when she'd moved in, and she didn't want him to lose any business because of her change of circumstances.

"Mr. Lawson?" she asked when he answered the phone. "This is Rachel Cason, that is, Rachel Crewes. I got married."

"So I heard. Congratulations."

"Thank you. I know this is short notice, but I've moved out of the house. Of course, I'll pay the rent for this next month, but Polly across the street has someone who wants to rent it, so my moving shouldn't be a problem."

The man chuckled. "Not for me. And I guess not for you, either."

Relieved at how easily he took the news, she said, "Thanks for being so nice about it. I know I have a lease, but—"

"Mrs. Crewes, since you're going to own the place now, I think you can let yourself out of the lease if you want, don't you?" He was still chuckling, apparently appreciating his little joke more than Rachel.

"What do you mean?"

"Oops, hope I haven't spoiled a surprise, but your husband called me Monday. He made me an offer I couldn't refuse and we're closing on the house tomorrow. He said he was putting it in your name. *And* he's paying cash. Nothing like landing in honey, is there?" Again he chuckled.

Rachel didn't feel like laughing. With her voice just barely above a whisper, she apologized for disturbing her former landlord and hung up the phone.

She stared across the kitchen table, her sandwich forgotten. He'd bought her a house. For when their year ended, of course. And as payment.

That ugly thought made her gag. She'd hoped last night might have some meaning to John. When he'd caressed her, she'd believed there was more to it than desire.

But then she'd never been any good at understanding men. She'd believed Jacey's father had loved her, too.

At least Dirk hadn't tried to buy her favors, making her feel like a prostitute.

She squeezed her eyes shut, hoping to hold back the tears that filled her eyes. John Crewes was not going to make her cry. He wasn't, she assured herself as her tears splashed on her sandwich.

After an hour of weary debate, Rachel had made her plans. Although her heart was breaking, she knew she couldn't stay with John. She had offered him her heart last night, but he'd only wanted to rent it. For a night, a lot of nights, a year. Then he expected her to move back to the house next door.

That would be convenient for him.

And a disaster for her.

She couldn't do it. Better to leave now, while the pain was fresh, instead of dying a little each day. There was no way she could pretend everything was all right. All three of them would be miserable if she tried that.

Jacey. Tears formed again, but she quickly brushed them away. Jacey would just have to accept that John wasn't going to be a part of their lives. Her little girl would have her first heartbreak at the tender age of five. Rachel hoped it would be her last, but her experience with men didn't make Jacey's future look good.

What a disaster. All because of show-and-tell. She would hate show-and-tell for the rest of her life. Because she'd mourn the loss of her love just as long.

The phone rang. She glared at it as if it were her enemy. The caller probably was her enemy. It could only be John.

"Hello?"

"Hi, sweetheart. Are you awake?"

She'd been right. It was John. The sexy burr in his voice almost brought her to her knees. "Yes."

"Rachel? Is anything wrong?"

"No."

He paused, but when she remained silent, he said, "Maybe you'd better take a nap. Because tonight *I've* got a surprise for *you.*"

"More presents?" she asked tonelessly.

He didn't seem to notice. "Why not? You gave me a pretty special gift last night."

"I didn't ask for anything in return," she snapped.

"You *do* need a nap. And even if you didn't ask for this present, I think you'll like it."

Before she could respond, he had another call. "Gotta go, sweetheart. I'll be home as soon as I can."

Which meant she didn't have all that much time. Spurred on by the ache in her heart, Rachel ran up the stairs and began packing bags for both her and Jacey. She couldn't remove all their belongings before it was time to pick up her daughter, but she could gather enough things for several days. They'd go to a hotel until she could find them an apartment.

At least she wouldn't have to worry about the lease she'd signed on the house next door. All she had to concern herself with was two broken hearts.

When she picked up Jacey at her school, her child's bright smile almost started the tears all over again. She fought them off. She'd already cried enough today. Driving in silence, she listened to Jacey's chatter about her day, scarcely registering her words.

As soon as they got home, she made sandwiches for the two of them. Since she hadn't eaten the soggy one she'd fixed earlier, she forced herself to chew a few bites, but there was no taste; or if there was, she didn't notice it.

"Can I have some strawberry shortcake, too?" Jacey asked as she ate her sandwich. "And why aren't we waiting for John?"

"John's busy. And we're going to have a treat, you and me," Rachel said, hoping to instill some pleasure in her voice but failing miserably.

"A treat?" Jacey asked cautiously, watching her mother.

"Yes, a treat. I'll get you some dessert, now."

Her attempt to distract Jacey with the strawberry shortcake didn't work. "What kind of treat, Mommy?"

"I thought we'd go stay in a hotel for a few days."

"A hotel? You mean Disney World?" Jacey asked eagerly. "I didn't think we'd get to go!"

"Disney World? What are you talking about, Jacey?"

"Lisbeth said her parents were taking her to Disney World, and I said we were going too, but—" She broke off abruptly as she stared at her mother.

"Jacey, that's not true."

The excitement fading from her little face, Jacey frowned and asked, "Then why are we going to a hotel?"

"I thought it would be fun."

"Is John going, too?"

"No! No, John's not going."

"Then I don't want to go."

No, she hadn't thought she would. Neither did Rachel. But they didn't have a choice. She couldn't remain as John's paid companion; and Jacey couldn't stay, either.

"I'm sorry, Jacey, but we have to go."

Again the phone rang.

"Rachel, I'm on my way home. Don't cook dinner."

"No."

"See you in a few minutes."

After hanging up the phone, Rachel picked it up again and dialed a number. "Polly? Could I bring Jacey over for a few minutes? Thanks. I'll be right there."

"Why am I going to Grandma Polly's house?" Jacey asked, a frightened look in her eyes that made Rachel unbearably sad.

"Because I need to talk to John alone."

"We're leaving him, aren't we?" Jacey whispered.

Rachel swallowed back her tears. "Come with me to Polly's, sweetie. I won't be long."

Jacey didn't ask any more questions.

After leaving her daughter with Polly, Rachel put their suitcases in the station wagon. She wasn't going to run away without telling John goodbye. He didn't deserve such shabby treatment. In fact, he hadn't done anything wrong. Except not love her. And he couldn't help that.

So she'd wait until he came home...with another present. And she'd tell him goodbye.

Chapter Eighteen

John whistled as he drove.

Life was good. What he and Rachel had shared last night would have made even the worst day a gem, but he'd had a good day. Rachel was going to be surprised when she heard what he'd done.

He patted his chest, just over his inside pocket. Yes, she was going to be surprised.

He wanted to buy her the world, to make every wrong right, to love her forever. And he had a year to convince her. He was starting tonight.

When he'd married the first time, he'd thought he knew what love was. He knew now he'd only known what lust was. Maybe some people got lucky, marrying young, but he hadn't. In a few years, when Jacey came to him and told her she was in love, he would have a long talk with her. Because love was something special, something incredible.

Last night, when Rachel had come to his bed, offering her body, he doubted that he could have turned her down, even if he hadn't loved her. But he did. He loved her more than he'd ever loved anyone. Even more than Jacey. And he'd been pretty surprised by his capacity to love a child.

The night spent holding Rachel, touching her, becoming one with her, had confirmed his feelings. Confirmed? He chuckled. Hell, it had set off rockets. It was a wonder the moon hadn't been blasted out of the sky.

Pulling into the driveway, he tried to wipe the idiotic smile off his face, but the thought of seeing Rachel again sent him out of control. Maybe Jacey could watch television for an hour while they, um, communicated. Then they'd all go to dinner.

He practically raced up the sidewalk, calling Rachel's name as soon as he crossed the threshold. When she appeared at the kitchen doorway, he scooped her up into his arms, his lips covering hers.

After a long kiss that only left him wanting more, he buried his face in her neck and whispered, "I missed you. Where's Jacey?"

"At Polly's."

He drew back, a grin on his face. "Terrific. We must've been thinking the same thing." Even as he turned to pull her toward the stairs and the bedroom above, he realized something. While Rachel hadn't fought his kiss, she hadn't responded like last night. Almost simultaneously, he recognized resistance in her body.

Stopping and turning around, he asked, "What is it? Are you sore? Did I hurt you in some way last night?"

"No." She pulled her hand out of his grasp and her teeth sank into her bottom lip.

"What's wrong? Has something happened to Jacey? Dear God, is Jacey hurt?" Panic filled him as his perfect world, less than twenty-four hours old, began to crack.

"Jacey's fine."

He reached out to grasp her shoulders and she stepped back from his touch. With painful intensity he studied her. "Tell me what's wrong, Rachel."

She ducked her head and then looked up at him. "We're leaving."

Pain was in her eyes, tension in her body. Her words struck him like a bolt of lightning. He couldn't move. But he managed to asked the one thing he had to know. "Why?"

"I can't stay," she whispered.

"What did I do that was so terrible? I thought—last night we— Damn it, Rachel, tell me!" This time he grabbed her shoulders and hauled her up against him, but she shrank back, as if his touch was distasteful.

She kept her head down. "You didn't do anything wrong. It's me."

He squeezed his eyes shut, hoping to hold back the unexpected tears that filled them. How could he lose her now? She'd promised him a year. He'd made such plans for the three of them—his family.

In spite of her reluctance, he pulled her close and wrapped his arms around her. "Rachel, please, don't go. You can't go."

He felt more than heard the sob that broke from her. What was wrong? If she didn't want to go, why was she leaving? Nothing made sense anymore.

"I don't understand," he added, a desperate plea in his voice.

She pushed away from him. "What did you bring me today?"

"What?"

"You said you brought me a surprise." She looked at him now, big tears streaming down her cheeks.

"Rachel, what difference does it make? If you're leaving, what the hell difference does it make?"

She sniffed and stiffened her shoulders. "I just wanted to see how grateful you were. It couldn't be bigger than buying me a house, but since I gave you what you wanted last night, I figured it would be spectacular."

Stunned, he couldn't respond. He stepped back, staring at her.

"You've said you're rich, and you must be. But I'm not sure even you could afford a year's worth of payments like the ones you've made so far. I thought I'd save you from bankruptcy," she said, her voice hardening, anger beginning to fill her face. "And here's a word of advice. For your next mistress, you'd better start off cheaper. Then maybe you can last the course."

As soon as she finished speaking, she moved to step around him. By the time he pulled himself together and turned, she was almost to the door. But he beat her there.

He drew a deep breath, trying to bring himself under control when all he wanted to do was shake her until she forgot her foolish thoughts.

"Please move," Rachel muttered, standing rigidly in front of him.

"Aren't you going to pack a bag? Take your toothbrush?"

"They're in the car."

"Ah. So you've been thinking about this all day. That's why you sounded so mad over the phone." He shoved his hands in his pockets to keep himself from grabbing her.

"Move."

"No. I'm not going to move until you hear what I have to say. Surely it's only fair to let the accused speak up for himself, isn't it, teacher? And you believe in fairness, don't you?"

She was rip-roaring mad now, and shaking so much he feared she'd fall. "Yes! Yes, I believe in fairness. But I don't believe in treating a person like a commodity that can be bought and sold. And—and I don't believe in breaking a little girl's heart." Sobs racked her body as she looked away.

"Jacey knows?"

"She—she guessed."

"Damn! How could you do this?"

"I can't stay!" she shouted. "How can I stay, when—when you don't care?"

For the first time, real hope filled John. Why would she want him to care unless she cared, too? He should have known, he realized, his heart rebounding with ferocity. He should have known Rachel couldn't have made love with him last night unless she cared.

"Oh, Rachel." He sighed. "I never said I didn't care."

"It's too late," she protested, sobbing. "Let me go, John. It will destroy me if you don't."

"And it will destroy me, if I do. I love you, Rachel. You promised me a year. I want my year to prove that I love you and Jacey. We belong together."

His hands came out of his pockets, and he gathered her against him. She didn't have the strength to fight him, shaking as much as she was. "No, no, no," she protested, but she buried her face in his shirt.

"Rachel, as God is my witness, I love you—more than I ever thought I was capable of loving anyone. I love you more than all the money in the world. More than life itself. I even love you more than I love Jacey."

She lifted her head and stared at him, the faintest light of hope in her big blue eyes. "What?"

"I love you."

"But—but you bought the house next door for when our year was over. You didn't plan on our marriage lasting."

"I bought the house next door because you didn't seem to want to give it up. I figured it would be a good investment."

"You put it in my name."

"It's your house."

"That's crazy," she said, hiccuping.

For the first time since he'd realized something was wrong, John smiled. Not a big smile, just a rueful grin. "I'm crazy in love with you."

"John, please, if—if you're just saying these things to protect your company, tell me now. I'll write David a letter and explain that it's my fault. That you are the perfect husband. But don't lie to me."

John looked up at the ceiling as he pressed Rachel against him. "Can you believe this woman, God? She won't even take *You* as a reliable witness. I'll try again, sweetheart. May God strike me dead if I'm lying. I love you with all my heart, and I always will."

Although she remained in his arms, she said nothing and he pushed her chin up so he could see her face. "Well?"

"Just a minute. I don't want to rush God. He could be busy." There was a teary twinkle in her eyes even as her lips trembled.

It was more than enough invitation for John. He tightened their embrace and covered her lips with his. Heaven might be a wonderful place, but John couldn't believe it could be better than Rachel's kiss.

When he lifted his mouth from hers, he hugged her even tighter. "I thought I'd lost you, Rachel. You scared me out of ten years of my life."

She sobbed against his neck. "Me, too. I've been dying all day. I loved you so much, and then I found out about the house, and I thought—"

"You thought all the wrong things. Sweetheart, I can't help buying you things. I was trying to tell you I love you—not offering you a bribe."

"I'm sorry. I just— And when I told Jacey— Oh, no! Jacey!" She pulled out of his embrace and tried to open the door. "I've got to go to Jacey!"

"We'll both go to Jacey," he told her, taking her hand and pulling open the door.

They raced down the steps and headed across the street, where a very sad little girl sat watching them.

"I'M GOING TO SIT on the front porch and wait for my mommy," Jacey told Grandma Polly.

"But, child, she may be a while."

"I don't think so," Jacey said, turning away so Grandma Polly couldn't see the tears running down her face. She didn't think her mommy would take long to tell John goodbye.

She wished she could understand why they had to leave. Had Jacey done something wrong? She'd promise to be very, very good, if they could stay with John.

It had to be her. Her real daddy hadn't wanted to stay, either. Maybe John was tired of being a daddy. She sat down on the porch step, leaning her head against the post that held up the railing.

She wished he still wanted her to be his little girl. He'd been such a good daddy. The best.

Hearing the door open at John's house, she watched as the two most important people in her world tumbled down the steps and rushed toward her. She frowned. They were holding hands.

Hope leaped in her, but as they got closer, she could tell her mommy had been crying. As much as it hurt, she couldn't let John make her mommy cry.

She stood and hurried down the steps to grab her mommy's leg. "It's okay, Mommy. John won't make you cry anymore. I won't let him."

She gave him a fierce glare, although her heart was breaking as he knelt down beside her.

"Good for you, Jacey," he said softly, a grin on his face. "You're a good girl to protect your mommy."

"Why did you have to make her cry?" she asked sadly. "You must've been really mean, 'cause my mommy never cries."

"Jacey, sweetie," her mommy said, kneeling too, her arms around Jacey. "It's my fault. I thought—I thought John didn't love us."

She looked at her mommy with a frown. "A'course he loves us, Mommy. Anybody can see that."

"You know, Jacey, sometimes children can see better than adults. Our eyes get tired and we miss the important things." Her mommy reached out to touch John's face. "You know we said we were just going to be married for a year? Well, John wants us to stay forever. Is that okay with you?"

"Are you sure?" Jacey asked John, turning to face him. "'Cause it would make us both cry a lot if you changed your mind."

"I won't ever change my mind. I'll be your daddy forever, sweetheart, if you'll have me."

She threw her arms around his neck. "Yeah! And maybe we can even get a baby." She giggled with excitement.

"I wouldn't be surprised," John said, scooping her up into his arms.

"John!" her mommy protested, but Jacey didn't think she was mad, 'cause she was smiling real big.

As long as things were going so well, Jacey thought she should ask for one more thing. "And maybe we can go to Disney World with Lisbeth?"

John jerked to a halt, and Jacey screeched and grabbed his shoulders, afraid she'd fall.

"How did you know?" he asked.

"What's she talking about, John?"

"Uh, that's part of my surprise."

"Going to Disney World?" Rachel asked, stunned. "But I have to teach summer school."

He grinned. "That's another part of my surprise."

"John Crewes! What have you done?"

"You folks okay?" Polly asked, stepping out onto the porch.

"We're terrific," John assured her. "Thanks for watching Jacey for us."

"Glad to do it. And glad to see she's happy again."

"Yeah. We're all happy now." John put an arm around her mommy's shoulders. "Come on, you two. We'll finish our discussion later. Right now, it's time to go home."

Jacey beamed. Time to go home. Because now they were a real family.

And they were going to Disney World!

Weddings by DeWilde

Since the turn of the century the elegant and fashionable DeWilde stores have helped brides around the world turn the fantasy of their "Special Day" into reality. But now the store and three generations of family are torn apart by the divorce of Grace and Jeffrey DeWilde. As family members face new challenges and loves—and a long-secret mystery—the lives of Grace and Jeffrey intermingle with store employees, friends and relatives in this fast-paced, glamorous, internationally set series. For weddings and romance, glamour and fun-filled entertainment, enter the world of DeWilde...

Twelve remarkable books, coming to you once a month, beginning in April 1996

Weddings by DeWilde begins with
Shattered Vows
by Jasmine Cresswell

Here's a preview!

"SPEND THE NIGHT with me, Lianne."

No softening lies, no beguiling promises, just the curt offer of a night of sex. She closed her eyes, shutting out temptation. She had never expected to feel this sort of relentless drive for sexual fulfillment, so she had no mechanisms in place for coping with it. "No." The one-word denial was all she could manage to articulate.

His grip on her arms tightened as if he might refuse to accept her answer. Shockingly, she wished for a split second that he would ignore her rejection and simply bundle her into the car and drive her straight to his flat, refusing to take no for an answer. All the pleasures of mindless sex, with none of the responsibility. For a couple of seconds he neither moved nor spoke. Then he released her, turning abruptly to open the door on the passenger side of his Jaguar. "I'll drive you home," he said, his voice hard and flat. "Get in."

The traffic was heavy, and the rain started again as an annoying drizzle that distorted depth perception made driving difficult, but Lianne didn't fool herself that the silence inside the car was caused by the driving conditions. The air around them crackled and sparked with their thwarted desire. Her body was still on fire. Why didn't Gabe say something? she thought, feeling aggrieved.

Perhaps because he was finding it as difficult as she was to think of something appropriate to say. He was thirty years old, long past the stage of needing to bed a woman just so he could record another sexual conquest in his little black book. He'd spent five months dating Julia, which suggested he was a man who valued friendship as an element in his relationships with women. Since he didn't seem to like her very much, he was probably as embarrassed as she was by the stupid, inexplicable intensity of their physical response to each other.

"Maybe we should just set aside a weekend to have wild, uninterrupted sex," she said, thinking aloud. "Maybe that way we'd get whatever it is we feel for each other out of our systems and be able to move on with the rest of our lives."

His mouth quirked into a rueful smile. "Isn't that supposed to be my line?"

"Why? Because you're the man? Are you sexist enough to believe that women don't have sexual urges? I'm just as aware of what's going on between us as you are, Gabe. Am I supposed to pretend I haven't noticed that we practically ignite whenever we touch? And that we have nothing much in common except mutual lust—and a good friend we betrayed?"